THE WANDMAKER'S APPRENTICE

MITCHELL TIERNEY

THE WANDMAKER'S APPRENTICE

MITCHELL TIERNEY

The Wandmaker's Apprentice

Published by Ouroborus Book Services
www.ouroborusbooks.com

Cover Design by Sabrina RG Raven
www.sabrinargraven.com

CHAPTER ONE
THE STREETS OF YORKTOWN

Claude ran as fast as his feet would allow him. The cobblestones were cold and uneven. He wove through the bazaar, ducking and weaving through markets, over the top of wooden crates and through roads packed with Clydesdale horses. They saw him and raised their front hooves, slamming them down hard on the stone ground.

'Hey!' a rider yelled at the young boy. 'Watch where you're going!'

'Sorry, Sir!' Claude yelped, dipping his cap to him.

He pressed his back against the brick wall and quickly caught his breath. Sweat beaded on his brow so he took his flat cap off and wiped his forehead with the back of his sleeve. His shirt was covered in holes and his pants were dirty. His boots were stitched together with string and fishing line. The importance of his task suddenly struck him, and he sucked in a lungful of air and started running again.

The journey took him through the streets of Yorktown, past the church where Father Jacob was hanging his clothes on the back line.

'Why in such a hurry, Claude Wells?' he yelled, as Claude zipped passed him and leapt over the fence.

'It's father!' Claude yelled back.

Through alleyways lined with trash and slop

buckets, Claude made his way to the end of town where a small building stood amongst the taller houses. On the door was a red cross, the paint peeling and faded. He stumbled the last few steps, his lungs squeezing and gasping for air. Up the stairs, he finally paused, raising his fists and banging on the wooden door. A woman answered quickly.

'Why are you bashing on my door? Are you trying to turn it into kindle?'

'It's… my… father,' Claude begged.

'Get up boy, I can't have you gasping and sweating on my front porch. Come through quickly.'

The woman, who was dressed all in white, and wearing a nurse's cap, took him through a room full of people lying on beds. Most of them had handkerchiefs covering their mouths. They were all coughing and looked gravely ill.

'Sit here. I will fetch the doctor.'

'But!' Claude said, leaping to his feet.

'Sit!' she demanded and pointed to the chair.

Claude sat, but was unable to keep still.

Suddenly the Doctor appeared. He had blood on his apron still and his hair was dishevelled.

'What is it boy?' he yelled. 'I'm in the middle of surgery!'

'It's father… he's not well again.'

The Doctor looked towards the door, as if expecting to see him standing there. He looked back at the young boy.

'I'll be there when I can.'

'No,' Claude said, rushing over to him. 'Mother said it's bad this time. You must come now.'

'Okay,' the Doctor nodded, looking down at the small boy in his ragged clothes. 'After I sew this man's leg up, if he hasn't lost too much blood from me being out here conversing with you, I'll come by.'

Claude saw the woman reappear, as if her and Doctor weren't allowed to be in the same room at the same time.

'Thank you,' Claude said as he headed towards the door.

'Tell your mother it will be 4 shillings!'

Claude pushed on the door and didn't look back. He ran into the street and up through the alley way. There were people heading down from the township to see the Doctor. They were all coughing and spitting. Claude didn't know how they were going to pay the Doctor to come out to see them.

He headed towards home, going faster than he had before.

CHAPTER TWO
THE SICKNESS

Claude sat beside his father's bed and watched his mother dampen his brow with a wet cloth. His sweating was profuse and relentless. His father complained about the heat, even though the air in the small house was chilly.

His mother picked up a jug of water and poured a little into a glass. She lifted his head and he sipped it, before spitting it out over his drenched sheets and coughing wildly.

'When did he say he would be here, Claude?'

'I don't know. He didn't say. He was fixing a man's leg.'

Claude stood up and looked at his father. He was pale and his eyeballs had receded into their sockets. He looked ghastly.

'Get the last of the bread,' his mother told him. Claude did as he was told and ran to the kitchen. It was small, with shelves with no doors and a cooler box with no ice. There was a bucket of filthy water and flies buzzing around old onion skins. Under a small cloth was two slices of bread from a loaf they had brought weeks ago. Claude picked them up as if it was the last piece of bread on earth and took it back into the room. His mother took them from him and tried to feed it to her husband, but he refused.

'You eat it,' he told her. 'Do not waste it on me.'

'It's not a waste,' she told him. 'Not if you get well.'

'What if I don't get well,' his father said, followed by a violent cough that produced mucus on his lips.

There was a harsh banging on the door and Claude looked at his mother, who appeared afraid. He jumped to his feet and bolted for the door, swinging it open. Doctor Herbert stood on the doorstep. His shirt was stained with red and he was carrying his medical bag. He looked unpleasant.

'Are you going to let me in, boy? Or should we wait till your father passes into the next world?'

Claude moved aside and the Doctor rushed in, looking around frantically.

'They're in the bedroom,' Claude announced, pointing to the end of the hall.

The Doctor marched forward into the room, shutting the door behind him. After a little time, Claude could hear his mother crying. He crept slowly towards the door and pressed his ear to it.

'…the sickness. There is no cure. Only rest and water and pray that it passes. I can give him something for the pain, but he is in a bad state.'

Claude knew they didn't have 1 shilling to pay for the medicine, let alone 4 shillings for the home visit.

'I'll return in a week. If he gets worse, send the boy.'

The door swung open and Claude nearly fell into the room. The Doctor looked down at him with narrowed eyes.

'Eavesdropping, boy?'

'Will my father get better?'

'He needs the right medicine and clean water,' the Doctor looked around the room and marched back towards the front door. Claude followed him.

'If he can't work, then you must,' the Doctor told him.

'I can't. I'm only 14. Apprenticeships start at 16.'

Doctor Herbert leant down, so he was face to face with Claude.

'Ever heard about lying, boy. Either you bring in money, or....' Doctor Herbert looked over his shoulder at the room at the end of the hall. 'Tell the employment office I will vouch for you.'

Far down the hall he could hear his father coughing and splattering. The Doctor stood back up and stomped out of the house. Claude shut the door and slumped down to the ground.

That night, his father got worse. Due to the house only having one room, Claude slept in the small nook in the evening room where the fireplace was. There was no wood and it had not been lit for some years. His blanket was an old rug he found in the alleyway in town. He slept on rags for a mattress and his pillow was a balled-up shirt his father never wore anymore. The window above him let in moonlight. From where he lay, he could see the stars. They seemed so far away and, no matter how much he focused, he still couldn't see what they were. He heard footsteps coming down the hall. It was his mother. She fetched more water from the bucket and returned to the room. She had been awake now for over two nights, keeping vigil over her husband. What the Doctor had said to Claude had resonated with him. It rattled around his skull like a loose marble. *Tomorrow,* he thought, *I will go to the job market and look for an apprenticeship. I will lie about my age and get father the medicine he needs.* He closed his eyes and thought no more.

CHAPTER THREE
TO MARKET

Claude woke with his mother sleeping on the single armchair beside him. Her arms were wrapped around her knees and she was perched like an owl. He was going to wake her but decided she would need her sleep. Slowly, and careful not to make noise, he crept down the hall to see his father. He was asleep, snoring gently. The sheet was pulled up to his neck and a wet towel was over his forehead. Claude turned to leave him in peace.

'Claude?'

He looked back and saw his father looking at him through shallow, yellow eyes.

'Sorry if I woke you. I didn't mean to.'

'Come, sit.' Claude did as he was asked. 'You didn't wake me. I barely sleep as it is. A few minutes here and there.' His voice was harsh and struggled.

'How are you feeling?'

'I feel as if I'm...' he chose his words carefully, 'gaining some strength back. But it's still painful to move. My joints feel like they are made from iron.'

'I'm going to the market today to find an apprenticeship.'

His father glared at him with a tear lingering in his eye.

'An apprenticeship? You are not old enough.'

'Doctor Herbert said he would vouch for me. I'm willing to work, father. I *must* work.'

'No, Claude. Soon I'll be able to move… I'll be able to get back to the mine, pick up my old shifts and bring in money.'

'Father,' Claude said, his heart breaking a little. 'The mine closed a year ago.'

His father looked up at the ceiling, letting the tear roll down his cheek and into his beard.

'It'll be okay. I'll be okay.'

'You don't have to Claude. I will be up on my feet…soon. I'll find work.'

They sat in silence for a moment, just letting time pass together in the same room. It felt like death was lingering, and by being together, they were keeping it away.

'In my closet, there,' his father finally said, pointing in front of him. 'There is a white shirt. It has buttons. Some old pants. Both will be too big for you, but they will do. Wear shoes and comb your hair. You're a polite boy, so you should have no problems getting an… apprenticeship.'

Claude stood up and opened the closet. There was hardly anything in it. Hanging over a wire line was the shirt. It stunk of old wood and moths. He pulled it down.

'I will get mother to iron it.'

'If… there is a choice,' his father said, fighting back a cough. 'Go for a baker. Bread is always in demand. A butcher, he can run out of pigs… Something that people need.'

'Okay. I'll let you sleep now,' Claude said, taking the shirt and heading to the kitchen.

He ironed it the best he could, burning the back a little. He left his mother to sleep further. He fetched his trousers, that had a hole in each knee and borrowed his fathers' belt. The last hole was just enough to keep them on his waist. He slid his shoes on and wet his hair with the water in the bucket. There was no brush or comb, so he used his fingers to push his shlock of blonde hair back. He closed the door with care and ran.

Something in him always wanted to run. He knew the city well enough to take every shortcut imaginable. Through the church yard, over Peter O'Dooley's fence where he kept chickens and down the alleyway with all the trash. He could smell the sea, as well as freshly caught fish and could hear the howls of feral cats begging for scraps. He was close. As he rounded the bend in the road, he came face to face with a large black stallion. It reared up on its hindquarters and neighed like a malevolent beast. The rider wore a long black cloak, equal in colour to his horse.

'Whoa, whoa… steady, boy,' the rider said. The riders hood momentarily slipped from his head, revealing a metallic mask that covered his jaw and dome of his head. His eyes looked pale green through the metal. 'Careful where you run, boy. These horses can't see rodents like you.'

Claude stepped back, out of the way, as the horse steadied itself and galloped on its way. Behind it, a long black carriage was being pulled by two equally huge horses. Their chains were glittering silver and their buckles looked freshly polished. When they had passed, Claude bolted across the street and into the market bazaar. There were aisles upon aisles of fresh produce, some stinking and old and others still covered in fresh soil. People were shouting and doing deals with local restaurant owners, others were haggling without any luck. Claude never came to the market. There was no need. His family didn't have money for fresh vegetables, and it only made his stomach rumble if he looked at it.

He made his way along the long, muddy, footpath until he reached a small outcropping of buildings near the port. Over a rather crooked, rotten, door was a sign that read *Jobs and Hire*. He straightened his shirt and looked at himself in a puddle of muddy water to make sure his hair was slicked back, then entered the building. Inside, there were men lined up in front of a long counter. Three in total. They all looked like sailors looking for a deck-hand job. They had steely eyes and ragged, sea-breeze hardened flesh. Their hands were large and covered in scars. They smelt like the ocean and the land, both at once. Claude lined up behind them. They were all at least 2 or 3 feet taller than him with heavy set boots and tough leather belts. The man in front of him turned and glanced down.

'You won't make much of a ship hand, with those

puny arms,' then he started to laugh. The other two men in front of him looked at the commotion and hunched over in laughter. Claude didn't seem to mind. His arms *were* skinny, and he wasn't here for a sea hand position anyway. The smell of fish and the rocking of the boat would make him too sick to be useful.

To his left was a figure sitting on a long wooden bench. His leather boots were caked in mud and his long, black cloak was mattered in the same dried soil. His hands poked out of sleeves, showing long spindly fingers, each of which wore a ring. His skin was wrinkled and veiny. From under his hood was a long, grey beard. It was thick around the chin and cascaded down, nearly to the floor. On the table in front of him was a feather and ink pot. The man squiggled something and stood up suddenly. Claude was impressed by his speed. He walked over to the counter and slid the Jobs Attendant the paper. He checked it, nodded and thanked him. On the way out, the cloaked man stopped by Claude, who looked up at him. His face was nearly completely covered in shadow, except his eyes, which were stone-cold silver. He nodded and Claude nodded back, feeling a lump stick in his throat.

'Next!' The Jobs Commissioner yelled.

Eventually, Claude got to the front of the line. His feet started to hurt due to the shoes he was wearing being a size too small and standing still for quite some time. The man behind the desk looked at him, licked the end of his feather-pen and glared at the young boy.

'If you're after a handout, we don't do that here. Go see the tax office. Next!'

'No, no,' Claude said, barely able to see over the countertop. 'I'm here to apply for an apprenticeship.'

The Jobs Commissioner looked down at him and narrowed his eyes. 'How old are you?'

'16,' Claude lied.

'Who's your father?'

Claude wasn't sure if he should run out of the store or answer the questions. 'Lonnie Wells.' The man squinted his eyes even further, which Claude wasn't sure had been possible. 'And your mother is…'

'Hilda Wells.'

'I see,' the man said, writing briskly on a parchment of paper. 'Your old man… he worked at the mines before they closed, correct?'

Claude nodded. 'Yes.'

'And your mother at the hospital?'

Claude hadn't known if his mother worked at the hospital or not. He had never heard her talk about it. He nodded nonetheless.

'What has your father been doing the last year?'

Claude wanted to sink into the floor. It was far too many questions. 'He's been ill.'

'Oh, I see.' The man stood up and waved him into the next room. As he passed the counter, he collected several pieces of parchment from a tray. The next room was small and had a jug of water with two pieces of lemon in it. 'Help yourself,' the commissioner said, waiving to the chair and then to the water.

Claude had never had water with lemon in it before. He poured a glass and drank it feverishly. The Jobs Commissioner sat down and looked through the pile of papers. 'Never too young to start bringing money into the family, that's what I say,' he said, licking his finger and flipping through the pages.

They sat for several minutes with the smell of the sea and call of the gulls coming through the open window. The aroma started to turn putrid and made Claude's stomach upturn. The Job Commissioner flipped through page after page, scratching his balding head and pulling at his feeble beard.

'And what sort of apprenticeship were you after, son?' he said, finally looking up.

'Well,' Claude pretended to think. 'Not a butcher, not a deckhand, but maybe a farm-hand? Or the sort?'

The Jobs Commissioner stared at him for some time. 'I don't have any of those left. Can you carry sheep?'

Claude thought he might be able to, but all the sheep he had seen had chased him out of the yard. He shook his head. As he was reminded earlier, even if he wasn't chased, his arms were still too small. The man got to the bottom of the pile and slowly slid out the parchment. He read it thoroughly and raised his eyebrows when he got to the end.

'Well this one only came in a few moments ago… are you good with wood?'

'I've chopped down plenty of trees,' Claude lied. He had only chopped down two trees in all his life. But, when they did have a fire, he would carry the wood inside.

'That will do. Please sign here.' He slid the parchment in front of him.

Claude could read a little, but not the whole page. It looked like cursive writing, but it was jumbled and full of squiggles and harsh lines.

'A carpenter, Sir?' he asked.

The commissioner lent over and placed the feather in his hand. It dripped small dots of ink onto the page.

'It pays two pence a week.'

Claude looked down at the page again. He hesitated for a moment, then thought of his father in bed. He needed to bring in money, no matter what the job. Claude had never signed anything in his life. He knew how to spell his name but didn't know cursive. He placed his name on the page as best he could and looked up at the commissioner.

'You start tomorrow. 6am sharp. Meet out the front here. We will tell the employer that you are arriving with your belongings.'

The Jobs Commissioner stood up and snatched the parchment away before Claude could rethink his decision.

'My belongings?'

'Yes, dear boy. This job comes from the next county – Shrub Oak.'

'Shrub Oak?' Claude said, sounding a parrot now.

'Isn't that...'

'Mr Crenshaw is getting old and his hands don't work like they used to. He needs someone to cut the wood and turn the wheel. That's it. It's a stay-in apprenticeship. You'll be allowed home once every ten days.'

Mr Crenshaw? Claude thought, standing up. He had hardly noticed the commissioner holding his hand out to shake it. Claude extended his right hand and the man almost shook it out of its socket. As he left the room, Claude was struck with the sudden realisation he would be leaving his sick father. The job agent saw his distress and turned on his heels.

'Look, boy. It's good money for a young lad. I was on less than that when I started. I can see you're not 16 yet, so I would take it if I were you. It's easy work and Mr Crenshaw is... well... nice.'

'I don't know, Mr...' Claude waited.

'Alistair.'

'Mr Alistair... the money does sound appealing, but once every ten days?'

Mr Alistair trotted into the hallway. Claude followed him, unsure if he should or not. They entered the last room on the right. It was a small, claustrophobic room with piles of paper and spilled ink wells. Mr Alistair lit a lantern, as the room was void of windows and started shuffling through the draws in his office. He slammed his hand down on the table, palm flat. He slid it over to Claude.

'Pay in advance. Now go. Gather your things and

be back here tomorrow. Wait out the front by the stool.
Don't be late.'

He removed his hand and two pence stared up at
Claude. He took them and ran home.

CHAPTER FOUR
THE IMPOSSIBLE TASK

'I don't know, Claude. I think I should meet this Mr Crenshaw first.'

'Mum,' Claude pleaded, as softly as he could so his father didn't hear him. 'This is two pence a week and I'll come home every ten days. I'll ask if I can come home sooner, if he allows me.'

His mother's face looked dirty. Her hair was strung up at the back of her head with a piece of string. Her clothes were ratty and full of holes and smudged with dirt. She held the two pence Claude had given her, but she looked as if she was going to give it back. He could sense his mother was at ends about the decision.

'If I don't like it, I'll come home. It isn't far. Mr Alistair said I'll be chopping wood and turning a wheel of some sort.'

Tears started to stream from her face. 'I'm sorry it has come to this, Claude. Will you say goodbye to your brother before you leave tomorrow?'

Claude looked at his feet. 'Yes. I will.'

That night, Claude could hardly sleep. In the matter of a day, he had gone from scavenging through old alleyways for food and clothes to being given two pence and a job. He could hardly believe his luck. He pulled his itchy blanket up around his neck and his feet slid out the bottom. He looked at his toes wiggling in the moonlight. Far down the hallway he could hear his mother and father talking. They were talking about him. He closed his eyes and tried to get some sleep before his big day.

The moon watched the empty streets as clouds shifted and waned. Rats and cockroaches scuttled for food as the sun began to rise. Slowly, the orange light drifted into the window and across Claude's feet. He opened his eyes in a flash and leapt from his bed. It felt as if he had only received a few hours sleep, but he didn't care. He washed his face in the remainder of the water and slipped into the same clothes he wore the day before. He fastened a bag to his back with rope and headed down the hallway. His mother and father were in the same bed. His father was snoring gently. He kissed him on the forehead and then went over to his mother. Her eyes were barely open.

'You come back when you can, you hear?' she said, taking his hand and kissing his palm. She then pressed his fingers into a ball.

'I will.'

Claude ran from the house and through the city into an open field of yellow daisies. He stood with the flowers up to his shoulders and watched the sun peak up over the mountains, as if to welcome him. He looked through the flowers for some time until he found the biggest and brightest one. He pulled it from the ground just as a barking voice boomed over the field.

'Get out of my field!' said a farmer, carrying a

rather large pitchfork.

Claude ran, knowing perfectly well the old man would never be able to catch him. No one could. He took a shortcut through Father Jacob's church yard. He could see a candle flickering in the outhouse. Mildew softened the ground, dampening his feet. As he approached the graveyard, he started to slow and then came to a full stop right outside the gate. It was chained shut and bolted with a lock.

'Come to say goodbye to your brother, Claude Wells?' a voice said behind him.

Claude didn't bother to turn around. He knew it was Father Jacob. He held a lantern and was still in his under-garments.

'How did you know?'

'Word gets around town, son. I've had to lock the gate due to vandals. You've got exactly ten minutes until you're late.'

'I'll make it. I can run fast.'

'I'll unlock the gate for you.'

Father Jacob sloshed through the muddy entrance and used a small key around his wrist, attached to a leather string, to unlock it. He pushed the gate open and waved Claude inside.

'Nine minutes now.'

Claude thanked him and entered. Heavy fog wrapped around the stone tombstones like cotton wool. Soft rain started to fall. As Claude walked through the cemetery, he could feel his clothes and hair becoming damp. He walked the track he had made a thousand times, the grass was starting to die, matching his foot marks. Suddenly, he stopped in front of a small tombstone. It read *Claus Wells*. He started at it for some time. *Eight years old*, it read. Loving son of Lonnie and Hilda Wells. Loving Brother of Claude Wells. Tears welled in his eyes as the rain became heavier.

He ran from the cemetery as Father Jacob emerged with an umbrella.

'Two minutes, Claude Wells!' he called out after him. 'You'll never make it,' he whispered, smiling to himself as he turned and went inside, out of the rain.

Claude thought his calves would tear from their bone at the speed he was going. He leapt over puddles and ran under wagons, through horse stables and atop roofs. He saw the port come into view and slid down a long rope attached to a pile of old anchors. He straightened his clothes and tried his best to ring out his shirt. He approached the Job building and could see there was no one there. He stood where Mr Allister had told him; by the stool. The rain was now mixed with thunder and lightning. It was so loud it made his ears rattle. Portmen were unpacking huge crates of fish and crabs. They had been up all night and looked disgruntled. He sat on the stool and waited.

Half an hour had passed, and he was still sitting in the rain. Water dripped from his face, down his nose and into the puddle at his feet. After a short time, the rain clouds started to move west, but the rain stayed. It became light and the thunder decreased and eventually stopped. Claude sniffed and knew his pack was soaked through, as he could feel it on his back. Another half hour passed and still no one showed. He wondered if Mr Allister would want the two pence back, he had given him in advance. By now, his mother would have spent it on bread, fresh water and maybe, if Dr Herbert allowed, a down payment on some medicine. Suddenly, the fog that had been at the cemetery began spreading out through the city, towards the port. Claude watched it inch its way towards the bay and out to sea. As his head turned to watch it, he almost leapt out of his skin. A man was standing by the door, under the canopy of the employment centre. He had an inky black cloak on, a hood over his face and a long beard that jutted out, then down. It was sopping wet. His hands were in his cloak and his eyes could barely be seen through the dark veil of his hood.

'Claude Wells?' he said, his voice soft and gravely.

'Yes. Yes, Sir,' he answered, leaping to his feet.

He flung the hood back revealing stone white eyes with a rim of cold blue. His pupils were midnight black and his nose was long and arched down towards his lip. He was bald, but upon his hairless head were several long scars. The scar tissue lit up like railroad irons when the lightning flashed before them.

'I am Abraham Crenshaw.'

'Sir? Mr Crenshaw… are you…'

'A raven arrived yesterday evening at my residence, informing me a person had taken me up on my offer as an apprentice.'

'Yes, Sir. That was me.'

Abraham turned his steely gaze to the door of the employment building, then back to the boy, who was shivering and cold.

'Two years I've been coming here to find someone to help me… you are the first to take my offer.'

Claude thought about this statement for a few seconds. He hadn't really had any other offers, and it was nearly forced on him, but he didn't want to tell Mr Crenshaw that.

'It's a pleasure to make you acquaintance, Sir.'

Abraham stepped quickly, his movements were like a shadow and his hands suddenly appeared. He was holding a great axe.

'Carry this and follow me,' he demanded.

The sun was now up, high above the mountains and more ships were coming in with their morning haul. Abraham Crenshaw stopped briefly by the port and looked out at the sea. Claude, who had to hold the massive axe with two hands tried to see what he was looking at.

'Are we waiting for someone else?' he asked.

Abraham didn't answer for a moment, then 'No,' he finally responded. He watched a large boat pull into the dock and throw rope to waiting ports-men. Several families ran from the boat and over the plank. Chickens in cages were carried off. Once Abraham saw the last of the families dock, he turned on his heels and flipped his hood back over his face.

They walked out of town without saying a word. The axe in Claude's hands were starting to blister his skin. It was getting heavier and heavier by the minute.

'Where is your wagon, Mr Crenshaw?' Claude asked.

'What wagon?' came the answer.

The terrain became increasingly more difficult to traverse. The hills steadily climbed, and the flat, well maintained cobble roads soon turned to dirt and stone. After several kilometres of walking Abraham suddenly stopped. He looked left through a thicket of tall oak trees.

'What is it?' Claude asked.

'An Alder tree,' Abraham whispered.

Claude looked through the forest. All the trees looked the same to him. Then, without warning, Abraham marched from the path and into the forestland. Claude wasn't sure if he was to follow or stay on the path. Once Claude started to lose sight of him, he quickly followed. The trees were tightly packed together, and their trunks were nearly as wide as Claude was tall. He tripped over the tree roots, nearly dropping the axe twice. Abraham moved through the trees like a serpent. He swept his legs and arms through the branches and overbrush, moving as if the trees were allowing him passage.

'Here,' he said, placing his palm on a tall tree before him. 'Cut this one down.'

Claude looked up at the trunk. It appeared to go on forever. Its branches resembled wings of some enormous creature ready to take flight.

'Cut it down?' Claude echoed. It would have taken a grown man most the day to cut it down. 'I can't do this on my own.'

Abraham looked at him. His facial features were hidden in the gloomy shadows of the forest.

'I'll be back by dusk to get you.'

'Wait!' Claude shouted after him, as he began to trudge further in the overgrowth. 'You're coming back at dusk? And you want me to cut down this whole tree?'

'Do you often repeat everything people say, lad?' he turned and melted away into the shadows.

Claude looked at the tree and the impossible task in front of him. He lifted the axe, now seemingly to weigh more than it did to begin with. He struck the tree half-heartedly. The axe blade bounced off it, without making a scratch. He looked up as the sun was peeking through the green canopy. It was already half morning.

CHAPTER FIVE
A VOICE FROM THE DARK

Claude looked at the blisters on his hands. They were bubbled and filled with liquid. Some were bleeding. The tree had a few slash marks in it, but nothing else. Claude rested with his back to the Alder tree. He was catching his breath as the clouds came over, threatening rain again and making the woodland darker. Several animals had come out to see what he was doing. He saw an owl perched high above him. It hooted and flew away. A small rodent, it could have been a rat or a squirrel, ran up the tree near him, but he was too exhausted to follow it. Soon the sun would start its descent down and he would need the tree to fall by then. Claude feared that if he didn't have the tree cut down, he would be taken back home and left at his parents' doorstep, without an apprenticeship. He stood up, picked up the axe and began again.

As the sun dipped, he felt his hands become wet with blood and busted blister skin. He would drop the axe in utter agony, then pick it up and continue.

The gash in the tree was nearly midway through. The tree had begun to moan and protest. It was falling, but slowly. Claude stood back, the forest now in nearly complete darkness and looked up at the tree. It made him feel awful for cutting it down and he hoped Mr Crenshaw had plans for this tree. He walked around the other side and began to chop it. Soon, he began to hear the snap and cracking of hardwood. He wasn't sure which way it was going to fall, so he readied himself. Two more deep cuts and the tree moaned like an angry whale, toppling from the sky above. Claude leapt out of the way as the tree fell, making a sound so loud and furious, it momentarily made him deaf. As it hit the ground, a cloud of dust and dead leaves were kicked into the air. Claude ducked as he was covered in soil and strands of moss. There was an eerie silence after the fall. The forest was mourning. Claude looked at his hands. It was so dark, he couldn't see the damage, but he knew it was bad. His shoulders ached like they had never before. His back was strained so much he could barely stand straight. He lifted the axe and sat on the tree trunk. Crickets and chirps from night creatures filled the forest. It was cold and he was hungry and thirsty. He waited in the dark.

Soon, he could hear the crunching footsteps of someone coming close to him. He kept one hand on the axe and looked with narrowed eyes into the dark. He could see something moving, but it wasn't moving like a person, but more like a creature on its hind legs. Claude was frozen with fear. He stood up and gripped the axe. He was now used to its weight and knew how to swing it without missing.

'Who goes there?' he yelped into the oily blackness.

'Calm down, lad, it's me,' came Abraham Crenshaw's voice from the dark.

He appeared in front of him, as if a black veil suddenly lifted. It frightened Claude enough for him to step back.

'Where have you been?' Claude said, his voice shaking. 'I've been out here with no water or food all day. I wasn't sure I was going to be able to cut this tree down.' Claude knew he was upset, and tried to hold his tears in. 'My hands hurt so badly.'

Abraham looked down at him and reached for his hands. He turned them over and examined them.

'This will not be the last tree you cut down, lad.'

'I'm sore and tired…' He wanted to finish his sentence with, *and I want to go home*, but caught the words before they slipped from his mouth.

'No one told you this apprenticeship was going to be easy. Your hands will get tougher, your back will become stronger and your shoulders will be like mine. Stop whinging and give me the axe.'

Claude held it out. It had some of his blood on the handle. Abraham looked at it, then walked the length of the massive tree and cut off a single branch. He threw it to the ground.

'Carry that and follow me.'

'No,' Claude spat, stepping back, away from the branch. Abraham stopped suddenly. 'Not until you tell me what we are doing and where we are.' Claude's hands were shaking.

'Lad, I will take you back to your town and drop you off at the dock, now pick it up.'

'No,' Claude stood his ground.

The pounding of a horse galloping suddenly thundered through the forest. Both Abraham and Claude looked towards the road.

'Get down,' Abraham whispered, pulling Claude down to the ground.

He crawled on his hands and knees, closer to the road. Claude followed, unsure if he was meant to. From the road came the roaring stampede of horses. The first one to pass was a giant black horse. Its mane was plaited, and it had leather strappings, and shining silver buckles. It raced past them at full gallop. The next two followed, riding like lightning through the night. The last horse came from behind. A giant Clydesdale. Its hooves pounded the ground like hammers on an anvil. The horse reared up and the rider calmed it by patting its neck with its gloved hand. It stopped, just short of where Abraham and Claude were hiding.

The rider spun his leg over the mount and landed on the ground with a heavy thud. Abraham hadn't taken his eyes off him.

'I've seen him before,' Claude whispered. 'At the market… his horse nearly ran me over.'

'Shush, boy.'

The giant man stood in long robes. He had a red sash for a belt and his hair was greasy and slicked backwards. He stared into the dark, as his horse lifted its front right hoof and struck the ground, kicking it up into plumes of dirt. The man stared and Abraham stared back. There was no sound of forest life for a few moments and Claude began to worry the man would come forward and other riders would return, sensing his absence. But the man turned quickly and mounted his ride, taking off in a cloud of dust.

'Who was that?'

'The man I feared would return some day.'

'Is that who you were looking for at the docks?'

'Aye. It was. They are already here.' Abraham stood up and watched the road to make sure they were not returning. 'Get the branch, and hurry. Don't moan about it. Just drag it behind you and follow me.

CHAPTER SIX
MIRROR THE FLAME

Night had well and truly set in when they suddenly emerged from the forest glen. Claude took several steps out of the line of oak trees and onto a worn path. In front of him was a wide road, big enough for two wagons to ride abreast.

Claude dragged the branch across the road and down a small embankment. Abraham marched forward without saying a word. Ahead of him he could see nothing but miles of forest.

'Are we walking through that forest?' Claude snapped.

'No. Just over that hill,' Abraham replied, without turning around to answer him.

Claude looked, but couldn't see any hills. It was far too dark, with only a little moonlight to guide them. He looked up at the stars and hadn't seen so many in his whole life. Some nights, when he couldn't sleep, he would sneak out to visit his brother and lie down beside his grave and talk to him while looking up at the stars, but they were never this bright. Abraham looked down the long and winding road, then in the other direction. He leant down and placed his palm on the dirt. Claude didn't feel like being snapped at again, so he didn't ask him what he was doing. They had walked for hours through the toughest landscape he had ever been through. His pants, which were already ripped and torn, were now full of bramble thorns and prickles. His shoes hadn't protected him from the ground foliage, so now his feet were cut and sore. His already painful hands were now throbbing with pain from dragging the tree branch and the axe. Abraham stood up, staring towards the left side of the road.

'Someone has been through here,' he whispered.

'Who?' Claude answered, thinking the statement was for him, but in fact, Abraham was telling himself.

Abraham looked into the darkness, as if it was staring back at him. 'No one,' he said at a whisper and continued crossing the road and down a path.

It led them through a jungle of vines and foliage until Claude could see a small hill cresting an indentation in a mountain. Over the hill, which was covered in a shortened green grass, was a cottage with several extensions haphazardly built onto it. It appeared as if a slightly mad person had pieced together portions of a house without taking much care for decorum.

'See, lad. I told you. Come,' Abraham instructed and veered left.

A trail of small cobblestones started by the hill and led down from the crest of the mound, winding and turning around shrubbery and boulders until it got to the front garden of the house.

'Do you live by yourself?' Claude asked, dropping the branch as they entered the front gate.

'I do, lad.'

It was a two-story cottage with a twisted and leaning chimney. The windows were caked in grease and smoke damage. The window frames were ornate and had faces carved into them and they were all painted green. Claude couldn't make out the detail in the dark. The front door was painted a dark blue with a huge iron knocker on it. Abraham pulled a ring of keys from his cloak and unlocked two locks before the door croaked inwards.

'Come in.'

Two bright eyes shone in the darkness beyond the door. Claude froze, looking into the black hallway as the eyes suddenly leapt for him. His hands went up to shield his face and he stumbled backwards, tripping on the welcome mat and landing flat on his back. The cat leapt onto his chest and looked at him bizarrely. It then started to clean its tail.

'For crying out loud, lad. Get up on your feet, it's just a damn cat.'

The cat stepped off the boy's chest and wandered into the front garden.

'That cat scared me half to death,' Claude said sheepishly.

'Well prepare yourself, lad. I have two others, now come inside.'

In the small foyer, there were piles upon piles of books. On the right wall were hooks, with several cloaks and beneath them, a pair of boots. The room was cold, even more so than outside. Claude followed

Abraham through to a small lounge room where there were two single seats and a table stacked with papers, candles and a rusted candelabra. The fireplace was red brick with scorch marks ascending to the ceiling. There was no fire, but piles and piles of wood haphazardly thrown beside it.

'Come through, boy.'

There was a black cat sitting on one of the chairs. Claude hadn't noticed it at first until it moved its head when Abraham spoke. One of its eyes was cloudy. It stood up and stretched, turned around in a circle and sat back down. From behind him, Claude could hear Abraham's heavy footsteps going up a wooden staircase. Claude rushed to follow. The second story was even colder. There was a long narrow corridor with paintings hanging on the walls. It was too dark to see who they were. They were all hung crooked or fallen that way and ignored. Abraham stopped and opened the first door on the right.

'This is your room.'

Claude looked inside. There was a cot made up, with a towel folded on the bed. There was also a clothes cupboard and a night table with a lantern. He looked up at Abraham.

'I get my own room?'

'Well lad, you're not sleeping outside. Put your belongings away and meet me downstairs shortly, I'll make supper. Tea and hot bread with butter.' Abraham turned away and disappeared down the hall.

Claude looked into his room before stepping into it. He had never had his own room. He slept in the lounge room his whole life, in a corner.

After a short time, he scurried downstairs and saw Abraham with his coat off, stoking the fire. His three red scars went all the way back over his head and down his neck. His shoulders were wider and after he had piled the fire with wood, he tried to stand, but moaned and cursed his spine loudly. The oak table was cleared and set out with a pot of tea, and bread, already cut. A slab of butter sat on butchers' paper. Abraham lit a lantern and placed it near the end of the table and sat down.

'As you can see, lad, my back and knees aren't what they used to be. Father Time has caught up with me and gripped tightly.' He looked over to him with steely grey eyes. 'Some things are becoming harder to do, and some impossible.'

'Yes, Sir.' Claude replied, gazing into the fire.

'The tree you cut down today, will be the first of many.'

'What are you making?' Claude asked, moving his glare over to Abraham.

The fire reflected in his eyes. He suddenly stood up and went to the draws lined up against the eastern wall. He slid the first one open and pulled out a long, dark-wood box and sat it on the table. It was rectangular and covered in inscriptions. Claude didn't recognise the language. Abraham slid the cover off. Inside was a beautifully carved wand sitting on a bed of soft silk. The wand was ashen grey with a waxy black handle. Lengths of string were wrapped around the base, with carved beads and small feathers.

'Wands,' Abraham answered, looking down and marvelling at his creation.

Abraham gently picked it up from its casing and held it to the firelight. The lantern on the table dimmed its light and the whole room appeared to sway. The air around the wand started to vibrate and move in a way that Claude had only seen on the open sea, like oil on water. Abraham handed it to Claude, who at first was afraid to take it, but once it was in his hand, he felt a surge of electricity pulsating through his body. His fingers tingled and the hair on the nape of his neck stood on end.

'I don't understand,' Claude said, his eyes stuck staring at the wand.

Abraham lurched over to one of the single chairs and let his body fall into it. His beard hung over his belt and down between his knees. His silver coin eyes glared and mirrored the flames.

'I don't suppose you have been exposed to magic, have you lad?'

Claude was able to pull his gaze away from the wand. Abraham looked sluggish and old in the chair, as if he was about to sink into it and never get up.

'Magic?'

Abraham shifted his stare back to Claude. He held the wand to his side.

'What you know about this world, isn't

everything,' he said. 'Once I show you, you can't ever unsee it.'

Claude sat down at the dining table, placing the wand back in its box. 'What is it that you are going to show me, Mr Crenshaw?'

'The magic that exists here. It's been here for as long as the trees and the ocean. But as time passed, it has been pushed underground. But there is a resurgence. It is growing and moving quicker than any city above ground. Places, things, people, they've all come together, lad. Uniting and gaining strength. Magic is real and it exists. Not only in the mind, or in the body, but in the wand. An instrument of magic. A guiding tool.'

The fire crackled and for a moment Claude felt as if the world had stopped moving.

'You're not a carpenter, are you, Mr Crenshaw?'

'Aye, lad. I am. I started when I was younger than you. My father was a carpenter, like his father before him. Tomorrow, I will show you the store and you'll see what I do. However, it is but a guise. Making wands is what I actually do. And I do it well.'

Abraham rubbed his swollen knuckles and looked at his fingers. The muscle had nearly receded away, leaving him with thin, bony fingers.

'And you are going to teach me how to make them?'

'Yes. I can no longer cut down trees or drag them to the shop, nor can I turn the lathe wheel.'

Claude looked at his bloodied and blistered hands.

He wasn't sure he was going to be able to either.

'Mr Allister said I could return in ten days, back to visit my family.'

'Yes, you may. I cannot accompany you, as my shop, be it carpentry work or wands, always keeps me busy.'

'Why have I never seen magic? Or this underground?'

'We keep it hidden. In time, son, you'll learn more. But for now, we are both tired. Retire to your room as we have a long day tomorrow.'

Abraham stayed seated, staring into the flames as they licked the sides of the chimney. Claude walked towards the stairs and turned back to Abraham. He was already asleep.

CHAPTER SEVEN
FEATHERSTONE ANTIQUITIES

Claude woke up on the floor. After several hours of lying on the bed, he finally had decided to move onto the floor, in front of his nightstand. He was used to the floor. The bed was far too soft. What woke him was the heavy footsteps of Abraham approaching his door. There was a heavy thud.

'Lad, you've slept long enough,' said his booming voice.

Claude got to his feet as the door swung open. Abraham was dressed in his heavy boots, long black cloak and rings on each finger.

'Meet me downstairs in a few minutes. Bathroom is at the end of the hall if you want to wash up. There are clothes in your cupboard.'

Claude looked down at his pants. It was the third day he had worn them. His shirt was filthy and had started to stink. He heard the pounding of Abraham's boots going down the stairs. As Claude was about to head towards the bathroom, a small ginger cat walked past his door, paused and turned around. It walked in as if it had never seen the room before. It proceeded to sniff everything, including Claude.

'Hello there,' Claude whispered to it, stepping over it to enter the hall.

He washed his face and his underarms and dressed

in the clothes that Abraham had stocked in his draw for him. They were black pants, not new, a long sleeve white shirt, that was far from white now, and his own cloak. He headed downstairs where Abraham was extinguishing the fire in the hearth.

'There is toasted bread and butter on the table, and tea. Be quick, we have to open the store shortly.'

Claude looked towards the table. There were two slices of freshly baked bread, still steaming and a slither of butter on a small plate. A large mug sat beside it. Plumes of hot steam rose from the tea. It smelt delectable, but unfamiliar. Claude ate it as quickly as he could, nearly giving himself indigestion. Abraham opened the front door, letting long rays of morning light flood in. Claude hadn't realised how overly full his house was. Books upon books lined each shelf, long strands of wood and shavings filled the floor. Paintings and maps were pinned to every square inch of wall. Red and black candles lined every available space. Claude placed the remainder of the butter into the ice box and rushed for the door. His boots were barely held together. Claude thought the mud he had trampled through may be the only thing stopping them from falling to pieces. Abraham shut the door and locked two bolts with two separate keys.

'Your cat came into my room this morning,' Claude said, as they walked.

'Which one?'

'A small ginger cat,' Claude replied as they marched up the embankment.

'Oka,' Abraham said, staring at the long, winding road in front of them.

Claude thought it was an unusually funny name for a cat. There was a cat that used to live at the port, he remembered. It was some time ago. Its name was Fish. The deck hands would throw it scraps till it couldn't eat any more. It would hiss at anyone who came near it.

'Where is your store?'

'In the town of Shrub Oak. Have you been there?'

'No, I haven't been anywhere.'

They walked till the trees became so tall the sky disappeared. The oaks and pine trees hugged the road until it nearly suffocated the worn and dusty path. Claude felt as if he wanted to ask more questions, but Abraham seemed distant, as if he was concentrating on something. Ahead of them came the noise of people talking. Abraham suddenly stopped.

'What is it?'

'Quiet, lad.'

'Are they dangerous?'

Over the small crest came a wagon drawn by two small horses. They docked their heads down and neighed pleasantly. The two drivers saw Abraham and Claude in the middle of the road, standing stock still and yanked on the reigns for the horses to stop. One of the drivers pulled out a musket.

'Who goes there?' he yelled.

'Townsfolk heading to Shrub Oak. We work at the carpentry store,' Abraham hollered back.

Claude noticed his hands clench together, then disappeared under his cloak. The man holding the musket rifle spoke quickly to the other driver. From the right-hand side of the wagon a door flung open and a woman poked her head out.

'Gabriel?' she yelled. 'Why have we stopped?'

'Ma'am, please stay in the wagon. We are just conversing with these gentlemen.'

The sound of hammering hooves pounding the road came from behind Abraham and Claude. Abraham spun around to see another wagon coming at them at full gallop. He grabbed Claude by the shoulder and yanked him out of the way. The wagon was pitch black in colour and pulled by two massive horses. Their manes were covering their eyes, but they still appeared to see where they were going. The driver of the black wagon stared at Abraham as they sped past. The sound was immense and frightening. They came so close to the other wagon the driver dropped his musket and nearly fell from his perch. A dust cloud swarmed passed them, settling gently at their feet. Abraham rushed to the wagon as the woman was stepping down from the cabin.

'Who in the forsaken was that!' she yelped.

'Ma'am,' Gabriel yelped, scurrying to reach her before Abraham could. 'Are you okay?'

'Stop fussing,' she snapped, waving him away. 'I want that driver's name! He will be locked up for such reckless driving.'

Claude approached slowly, unsure if he should

stay on the side of the road or not. Appearing from the wagon came a young girl. She wore an equally abstruse dress, with white-linen fabric frills and decadent, hand-stitched, bows. She wore white gloves and a choker around her neck with a pearl dangling from it.

'Mother!' she hissed, hiking up her dress to stand on the road. 'We are going to be late!'

'Hush, Avery.'

Abraham turned to Claude, who was looking at the young girl called Avery.

'Are you okay?' Claude said, stepping a few steps closer to her.

Gabriel gripped his pistol but didn't raise it. 'Close enough, son,' he said. 'Stay where you are.'

Claude had never seen a pistol before, let alone told to stay back by a man holding one.

'Come, lad,' Abraham said, marching around the wagon and back into the middle of the road.

'Wait,' the woman said. 'I am Mabel Featherstone, of Featherstone Antiquities. I overheard you say you are a carpenter?'

'Yes, Ma'am,' Abraham said, dipping his head slightly.

'Well, we have just opened a store in Shrub Oak hoping for a clientele with interest in rarities and oddities from all around the world and we are looking for cabinets and drawers. For your patience and kindness, I would like to come past your store for a quotation.'

'Yes, Ma'am,' Abraham said. 'Abraham Crenshaw. Crenshaw Cabinetry and Woodwork.'

'Pleasure, Sir. I will be sure to drop by.'

Gabriel helped her and Avery back into the wagon. He flicked the reigns with his wrists and the horses eagerly continued their gallop.

Abraham watched them continue down the path and over the hill. Claude watched him.

'Come, boy, we are now late to open.'

CHAPTER EIGHT
THE WANDMAKER'S MARK

As they entered Shrub Oak, Claude could see people everywhere dragging carts, packing fresh fruit and vegetables and making their way up, through the gates. The small city was alive with commerce. Small children played with a ball by the front gate as sleepy guards were eating breakfast from a makeshift bowl. They eyed the pair as they walked under the sign that welcomed them. Claude noticed the gates that had been pushed open were made of iron.

The city was full of chattering and horse traffic. Along the wide streets were merchants, beggars and upper-class aristocrats hurrying off to their busy day. Every road was paved with large cobblestones. They still radiated the cold night air and were slowly warming up in the morning sun. Each street corner had a lengthy pole with a lantern nestled at the top. The oil fuelled flame was already extinguished.

'Come, lad. Stop dawdling.'

Claude was only a few feet behind him, but he rushed to catch up to Abraham nonetheless.

As several wagons rushed past them, they turned down a side street and continued into the heart of the city. Claude could smell freshly baked bread and the pleasant smell of newly pressed sausage meat. As they wound their way down a small decline they got to a darkened area of the city. The surrounding buildings and homes kept the morning light away from this area. Claude looked up and on the corner of the street was a rather narrow building, with solid foundations of brick and mortar. Wooden beams were exposed through the grout. Hanging on semi-rusted chains above the door was a sign; *Crenshaw Carpentry and Woodwork.* As they approached it, Claude could see how grand it really was. He had never been in a big city, let alone worked in a building.

Abraham fetched the ring of keys from his cloak and sorted them in his hand till he found the right one. He jammed it into the door and shoved it to the side. With a heavy clank and a bizarre rattle, the door opened. Claude followed him in. The smell of wood oil and timber quickly filled his nostrils. In front of him was a massive showroom of cabinets, writing desks, chairs and commodes. Vanity tables with mirrors formed a wall down the centre of the room, with an isle on either side full of grandiose furnishings. Abraham lit a lamp by the door and strung it up on a hook on the wall.

'Come in, lad,' he ordered, flipping the 'closed' sign around to 'open.'

Abraham led the way through the showroom. Claude was amazed at the intricacy of the woodwork. Everything was polished to a perfect sheen. Towards the end of the room was a countertop. An unlit lantern sat on the left, with a ledger book in the middle. Abraham walked behind the counter and lit the lamp.

'Pull across the curtains and let some of the light in,' he instructed, while fussing under the counter. 'Wrap them around the hook and meet me in the back.' He then disappeared through a thin curtain that was strung up across a rear door.

Claude stepped around the cabinets and chairs and yanked the red velvet curtains across, wrapping them around brass hooks screwed to the walls. He went around the room and did it to all the curtains. The showroom suddenly came alive with detail. The smell and beauty were nearly overwhelming. He went back to the counter and pushed his way through the curtain into the rear room. There was a small landing, and then several steps leading down to a sunken office. A desk was pushed against the left wall and Abraham, who had taken his cloak off, sat at the desk reviewing several parchments of paper. He wore wire-rimmed glasses.

'There is a broom in the next room, fetch it and sweep the front room before we have customers,' he said, without looking up from his parchments.

Claude looked towards a strange archway door to the right. It was slightly opened and made of lengths of uneven wood. The doorknob and keyhole were rusted and nearly falling out of the frame. He walked slowly down the stairs and in through the archway. The room was nearly as big as the front showroom. Claude took a step back in surprise; it was filled with hundreds of rectangular boxes, all lined up in small cubic holes up into the ceiling. The pigeon-hole bookshelves were all marked and associated with different colours, starting from dark red, to light red, then to blue and purple and finally orange and yellow. Labels were loosely attached to each column. The cursive writing was hard to read for Claude, but he could make out the words *Healing, Fire* and *Water*. In the middle of the room was a wooden lathe. The machine had two ends holding up a plank of wood that had been partially rounded. At the end was several varying size cogs and wheels. Attached to one wheel was a rubber loop that went down to a foot pedal. Scattered along the bench top were curled pieces of wood shaving and various tools. In the corner, was the broom. Claude stepped lightly over the shavings on the floor and took the broom back to the archway, he glanced behind him, in awe, and saw a single wand sitting on one of the side tables. It was lined with red thread for the handle, with a long feather intertwined in it. Several beads and wax covered the tip. It appeared to move towards him. He stared at it, but it didn't move again.

'Did you get lost, lad?' Abraham said, suddenly appearing in the doorway. 'Ah,' he said, suddenly realising what Claude had been looking at. 'You will get to know this room as well as the front room. But I must ask you to keep this area a secret. If anyone was to ask about the extension on the building, say you're a young lad on an apprenticeship for cabinet making and know nothing more. Understood?'

Claude nodded. 'Yes, Sir.' He went out the front

and started to sweep the floorboards. He moved in between the vanities with large mirrors and nightstands, collecting the dust and cobwebs. It didn't appear to have been swept for some time. He brushed the dust and wood chips that had floated through the rear room, out the front door. He noticed quite a few people now mulling and loitering around the streets.

'Lad!' he heard Abraham yelp.

Claude rushed back to the rear room where Abraham was sitting in front of the lathe.

'Crank this handle there, to move the wood. Your arm will get tired at first, but soon enough you will be able to do it with no qualms.'

Claude placed the broom against the wall and stood to the side of the lathe. He could see it attached to the floor pedal, but it had been removed and replaced with a crankshaft. He gripped it with both hands and started to turn it. It was stubborn at first, but slowly started to get easier. Abraham picked up a metal file and began to chip away at the length of wood.

'Faster lad, unless you want to be here all night.'

Claude cranked if faster. He felt the muscles in his shoulder and arms yank and strain. Abraham yelled for him to go even faster. Claude used all his strength to spin the metal handle around and around as Abraham moved the file closer to the wood. Chips of timber started to fly off and soon the square piece became cylindrical.

'Stop,' Abraham said, much to Claude's delight. He

listened for a moment then leapt from his chair and marched out of the room and up to the showroom.

Two women had entered the store. They removed their day caps and had stopped to marvel at a tiger-oak dresser.

'Mrs Featherstone, our paths cross again,' Abraham said, his apron covered in wood filings.

Claude, covered in wood chips also, headed up the stairs, seeing that Mabel Featherstone was accompanied by her daughter, Avery.

'Yes, Mr Crenshaw. As per my word that I would come visit your store, here I am. You have several very beautiful pieces. Did you make them all?'

'Yes, Ma'am.'

'Well, once my shop is open, I'm sure I will come back as pieces made of this craftsmanship are hard to find.'

'Thank you, Ma'am. I'm happy to give you a tour of the showroom, we also do made-to-order cabinetry.'

'I see,' Mabel said, her honey-blonde hair falling over her shoulders. 'Did you know we are practically neighbours?'

'Is that so?'

'I am down the street, on the corner. It is the largest building I could rent in Shrub Oak. Apparently, all the large warehouses in this city are rented indefinitely. Come, Avery,' she waved her daughter towards the door. 'We just wanted to stop by and say hello and thank you again. I'm sure we will see more of each other.'

Abraham bowed his head. Claude watched them leave, seeing Avery wave to him as she was corralled out the door.

'What did she mean by all the large warehouses are rented indefinitely?' Claude asked, picking pieces of wood out of his hair.

'Strange,' Abraham replied. 'Several buildings have been empty for years.'

Abraham returned to his lathe, while Claude cranked the handle. They stopped for tea after an hour. Claude could barely lift the cup to his lips. The front door was pushed open again and a small man in a long hooded cloaked floated in. He went straight past all the woodwork and stopped short of the counter. Abraham got up from his seat and went to the counter to greet him. The customer didn't say a word, either did Abraham. The small man slid a piece of paper across the counter and Abraham took it.

'Just a moment,' he said, and marched past Claude and into the next room. He came back momentarily with a rectangular box and took it to the counter, removing the lid. The small man threw back his hood and stared down at it.

'Beautiful,' he said. 'It is to my specifications?' he asked, looking up at Abraham.

'Yes.'

'Very well,' the man noted and dug into his cloak, retrieving a small, beige, bag of money. He plopped it down on the counter, took the wand-box and left in a hurry.

Abraham watched the man leave but continued staring towards the door. 'If you're hungry lad, there is bread in the bread crock on the counter and butter and cream in the ice box.'

Claude was always hungry. He had just learnt to ignore the hunger pangs. He took the bread out of the pottery box and cut off two thick slices. He lathered them with copious amounts of butter and ate feverishly. Abraham was at the counter when the door chimed open again. Abraham didn't look up at first, instead, he shuffled papers under the countertop and filled the lantern with fresh oil.

'How can I help…' he said, looking up as his words came to an abrupt stop.

'Abraham Crenshaw,' the man said, with deep sunken eyes and large, boulder-sized shoulders. Claude glanced up the stairs and could just see the man's head. It was the same person who had passed them in the forest, the one whose horse almost trampled him. He would never forget those pale green eyes.

'What are you doing here, Ives?'

The man stepped forward. Now they were only a mere foot away from each other. Claude could feel the tension between them. It was dark and foreboding.

'I need something from you.' Abraham waited. His hands to his side, his fingers pressing into his palms, and releasing. 'I need you to build me a wand.'

'There are plenty of other wandmakers in the

lands… you will have to go to them. I don't make wands anymore.'

Ives turned his head to the side and motioned through the glass to someone outside. The door swung open and several figures marched in. Behind them, they dragged the short man who had been in the store only moments prior. Ives snatched the box from his hands and tore it open. He held the wand out in front of him. An exquisite magical conductor, finely chiselled and pre-set with spells and healing magic. Ives studied it.

'This is your marking, isn't it?' he said, peeling the handle cloth back and revealing a small incision in the wood.

'I am not making wands for you, Ives Aries.'

Ives held the wand with two hands and broke it in half over his knee, letting the two pieces fall to the ground.

'You were the best, Abraham. The best anyone had ever seen. Due to this fact, you will make me a wand, or there will be consequences.'

Claude only then had noticed that he was holding his buttered bread up to his mouth, but he hadn't moved it in some time. He put it down and went to the woodwork room, snatching the broom in his hand and creeping quietly up the stairs. He held it as if he was about to cleave an axe.

'I require a specific wand, unlike any other. No other wandmaker has the skills or necessary connections to witches in order to have it made,' he reached into his long cloak and pulled out a parchment of paper. He placed it on the countertop and slid it over to him. 'I require it in three days' time.'

Abraham looked down at the parchment. It was a script of necessary spells to be pre- charged, the type of wood to be used and several ornamentations that had to be included. His eyes widened. 'I am not making that wand. A black wand is illegal, and you know that.'

Ives shrugged. 'If you don't…'

Suddenly the door swung open again. Mrs Mabel Featherstone came marching in.

'Oh, Mr Crenshaw, I forgot to invite you to…' she suddenly noticed the store was full of people. Ives turned to eye her. 'Oh, I'm so sorry, I didn't know you had so many… customers. Mr Aries, we meet again,' she said, bowing her head.

Ives bowed back, without taking his eyes off her.

'My grand opening is in two nights time and I wanted to invite you and the boy. 7pm sharp.'

She turned to Ives and nodded her good-bye and subtly left.

'The boy?' Ives said, his lips peeling back from his teeth.

'Leave,' Abraham demanded, still unmoving from his spot. Claude took several steps up the staircase, his broom still clenched tightly in his hand. Ives saw him and grinned.

'I'll be back in three days' time for my wand, Abraham.' He turned and headed out the door.

Claude ran up the remaining few steps. 'Who was that? Do you know him? That's the man we saw on the road.'

Abrahams eyes were fixated on the door. 'He's an evil man, Claude. Utter evil. I thought he was long gone from my life.'

'Will you make him the wand he has asked for?'

Abraham looked down at the parchment once more. 'I may not have a choice.'

CHAPTER NINE
THE STORM FROM THE NORTH

On the walk home, it had begun to rain. Abraham pulled his hood up over his head. He looked as he did when Claude first saw him in the employment office. Claude did the same. Looking down at his frayed and half-ruined boots, he saw they were already covered in mud. He wondered how much longer they would last. As he looked back up, he noticed Abraham had suddenly turned left and was marching down a long embankment, by a river.

'I thought your house was that way?' Claude protested, chasing him.

A fierce thunderclap lit the sky in bright white. The trees shook and the storm suddenly intensified.

'We aren't going home,' Abraham yelled over the howling storm.

Claude looked down the path where Abraham was. He looked back to the road that led home. He swallowed his frustration and marched after him.

'Where are we going then?'

Abraham didn't answer. The ground became slippery and Claude stepped carefully around flowing streams of water overflowing from the river. Abraham walked as if he knew he wasn't going to fall, or he simply didn't care. The path, now almost completely covered in running water, took them along the river, where it abruptly changed course. Claude now found himself in a thick forest. The sky above was darker than night. The heavy storm clouds had come from the north and stopped over the county. The deluge of water strained through the forest canopy, hitting Claude hard against his shoulders and back. He dared not look down at his boots. If they were completely ruined now, he would have to take them off and walk barefoot.

The path led through the woodland for several more feet until it faded away into mud and forest detritus. Abraham climbed over branches and fallen trunks. He turned to make sure Claude was close by. Water seeped down from the awning of branches above them as another loud, deafening, crack of thunder lit the strangled trees. Claude covered his ears. His fingers felt cold pressing against his flesh. The sound of clashing lightning suddenly erupted around them as a tree several feet away was struck by lightning. Sparks of orange and yellow showered down on them as Abraham rushed towards Claude and took him into his grasp, shoving him out of the way as the huge tree came crashing down to the ground. Claude hit the ground hard, and it sent all the air out of his lungs. Rain splashed his face. He looked left and could see Abraham stuck under one of the trees branches.

'Mr Crenshaw!' Claude yelped, gaining his breath quickly and leaping to his feet.

He pushed against the trunk and Abraham tried to

crawl out from under it.

'Push, lad!'

The rain came down heavier, as the clouds momentarily rumbled above them. From beside him, Claude felt a presence. He turned to see an elderly woman standing on top of the ridge, slightly through the trees. Rainwater dripped down from his face, making him blink. He tried to wipe his vision clear, but it was no use. He turned back to Abraham, who was snapping branches off and tossing them to the side. Two hands moved into Claude's vision, he stepped back, gasping as the elderly woman, now right beside him, laid her hands on the tree. Lightning cracked overhead again, but Claude didn't flinch this time.

'Help me, boy,' she said, pushing the branch.

Claude didn't refuse. He used all his strength to move the branch off Abraham's leg. He scurried out and lay on his back, catching his breath and looking up at the falling rain. Claude lent over him.

'Are you injured, Mr Crenshaw?'

The woman leant over him also, her face partially in shadow from her long hair.

'Agnes,' Abraham said.

'Abraham,' Agnes said back to him. She held out her hand and Abraham took it, and he was pulled to his feet. Claude was impressed by her strength. 'Storm came over quickly from the north. It was unexpected. Something else is on its way.'

'That's why I was coming to see you.'

She turned her gaze to Claude. She was only slightly taller than he was, and she wore a black kaftan with a bright red scarf wrapped around her neck. It hung down to her chest. A thin, veiled hood covered the rear of her head. 'And who is this?'

Abraham pulled sticks and leaves from his cloak. 'This is my new apprentice, Claude Wells.'

She looked at him with warm eyes. Her black pupils were dilated, with dark, shadowy rims encircling them.

'Well,' she said. 'We can't get any more wet, but we may as well get out of the rain.'

Agnes walked ahead of them, leading the way. He walked beside Abraham, as he was limping slightly, but was trying not to show it.

'This was who we were coming to see?' he said softly to Abraham.

He nodded. 'Agnes Steelborn, Daughter of Trove Steelborn.'

These words and hereditary lineage were lost on Claude.

After a short distance they came to a small enclave where two large foothills met. Tucked in the corner and surrounded by shrubbery and thick oak trees, was a cottage. Soft smoke was billowing from the chimney apparently undamped by the storm.

Agnes didn't speak until they were inside. She left her scarf and hood on and sat in front of the fire, trying to dry her weary and old bones. The house smelt of ginger, onions and boiling soup. There was no second level, that Claude could see, only a make-shift bed in the corner and what appeared to be hundreds of herbs and dried leaves hanging from string from the ceiling.

'Where do you come from, Claude,' Agnes said, staring in the fire, slowly rubbing her hands together. Around her wrists were cherry-red beads, with silver clasps.

Claude looked at Abraham, then back at Agnes. 'Yorktown, Ma'am.'

She nodded casually. 'I've not been there for many years, but I hear it is growing rapidly.'

'Yes, Ma'am.'

'Good manners. Your parents taught you well.' She turned to him. 'Your father is ill.'

Claude stood up straight. His eyes widened and he could suddenly hear his heartbeat in his ears.

'How did you…'

'I am a witch,' she replied. 'There isn't much I don't know.'

Claude felt a tear encroach on his eyelid. Shamefully, he had not thought of his father's illness for several days. Abraham stepped around Claude and reached into his cloak, pulling out a sopping wet parchment of paper. He held it out for Agnes to take. She simply glanced at the paper, then turned back to the fire.

'I need your help building this.'

'I will not.'

'I know what it looks like…' Abraham tried to protest.

'I know what it *is*,' she replied, standing and facing him. 'A black wand. One for raising the dead.'

Claude looked at Abraham. The front of his own cloak beginning to dry.

'This man will not stop until he has one.'

'Ives Aries the Inimical Wizard,' her stone-grey eyes swept up to meet Abraham's. 'He is here for the Mage.'

'The Mage is…'

'Dead.'

Abraham sat down. His eyes closed and he was suddenly awash in thought.

'The Mage?' Claude asked, staying standing.

The witch turned to him, further caressing her beads with her long fingers. 'The Arch Mage of Winchester.'

'I've never heard of them.'

'You wouldn't have, lad,' Abraham said, keeping his eyes closed.

'The Arch Mage of Winchester was a powerful wizard that brought the first clan of witches from England over to this country. He set up colonies of mages throughout the land. Keeping them safe, due to persecution of our kind. In return, they had to do his bidding.'

'Persecution?' Claude echoed.

'Magic and magical users have been around since the dawn of existence. They have just kept to the shadows, for good reason,' Abraham ran his fingers through his long beard and reopened his eyes.

'What reason?'

'Because of people like Julius Oghast, Winchesters most powerful magical leader.'

'What happened to him? How did he die?'

Agnes looked to Abraham.

'We killed him.'

'He had brought the clans over to establish reign over this land, to ascertain a stronghold where he could practice his dark magic and create a world of chaos and fear. He grew tired of living in the underground.'

Claude was lost for words. He bowed his head and tried to process what had been told to him. The room was claustrophobic, but warm. The dried herbs hanging from the ceiling moved slightly in the breeze coming through the window.

'And you are making a wand for him, for Ives?' Claude said finally.

Abraham stood up, now semi-dry. He ran his hands over his scarred head.

'We will make him a flawed wand. It will buy us time at least before he realises.'

'He will know,' the witch, Agnes, replied. 'He has grown more powerful than your first encounter with him all those years ago. The storm from the north was not mother nature's doing.' Agnes paused for a moment, then, 'I will gather the ingredients and materials needed for the dark wand. I should have them in a day. If you make the structure, not out of Wenge, which is typical, but of Gaboon Ebony. A lesser replacement. It does not hold the spells as well as Wenge wood and will give us an advantage.'

Claude looked downtrodden. 'But if we make his wand…'

Abraham cut in. 'If we don't, we could put many more at risk. At least if we make him a faulty wand, we can have some control over the ritual. We can stop him from bringing Julius Oghast back.'

Abraham nodded, as if his word was final and headed for the door. Claude followed, feeling slightly deflated by the encounter.

'We will see you shortly then. Good -night.'

Agnes nodded her farewell and watched Abraham and Claude re-enter the downpour and head for the hills.

CHAPTER TEN
THE FIRST STRIKE

Claude had a restless sleep. He dreamt of his father calling out to him from his bed. When he woke, he was drenched in sweat. He was on the floor again, even though the evening had been cooled from the rain. He moved to the bed to sleep more, but it was no use. Having the window open slightly, wasn't much help. He pushed his hair from his face and stared up at the ceiling. He wouldn't be able to go see his folk for another few days, and he was worried. A gentle tapping came from his bedroom door, followed by soft scratching. Claude got up from his bed and opened the door to find one of the cats sitting, staring up at him. A ginger cat with long white whiskers and a stunted tail, licked its paw, then meowed loudly.

'Master Crenshaw said he had several cats,' he said to himself as the cat pushed its way through the open door. Claude bent down to pat it, but it hissed at him and jumped on his bed, insistent on immediately cleaning itself.

'That is Oka,' said the heavy voice of Abraham from the hallway. 'She has been with me for some time.'

Claude looked to Abraham, and it appeared he had had a restless night also. His eyes were bulged and deep within his skull. Bags of soft purple hung under his bottom eyelids.

'We have to walk far today to get the wood required and get to the store in time to open.' Claude breathed in deeply and held it. He had started to wonder what kind of apprenticeship he had gotten himself into. 'Get dressed and meet me outside. We'll eat breakfast as we walk.'

Claude went to the washroom and poured fresh water into the basin from a bucket. He washed his face and body quickly, then returned to his room to dress. The cat, Oka, was curled up on his bed, fast asleep. He peeled the mud off his boots the best he could and rushed downstairs. The fire in the dining room was out, but still smouldering. The front door was open, and Abraham was standing there looking through his ring of keys.

'Hurry, lad,' he said, handing him the axe.

They rushed through the front acreage of land, over the grassy ranges of the Wandmaker's estate, making their way down the hedged path and through the stone-paved walkway. The sun was just peaking over the mountains and the birds were chirping loudly, celebrating their find of an early worm. Claude's hands had only stopped hurting properly this morning, from the first tree he had cut down. The blisters had popped but still ached if touched. Carrying the axe, it felt almost lighter than it had been previously.

They walked the path that led to town, passing farmers with wagons full of produce to sell. They nodded their good morning but did not stop to talk. Abraham handed him a torn piece of crusted bread and some dried meat. He ate it with vigour as they continued walking. As the town came into view, they veered off a slightly worn path through the woodland. Far in the distance, Claude could hear the sound of a waterfall.

'The man, Ives Aries, he wants a black wand to bring back a magician?'

Abraham stopped walking, abruptly and turned to Claude. 'He wants to raise the Mage from a grave.'

'Where is he buried?' Claude asked sheepishly.

Abraham pointed towards the great wall surrounding the city. Far on the peak of the ever-growing city, was a cluster of buildings that stood out from the rest. A grand church was in the middle, with several steeples and flying buttresses. Long spires raised into the air, covered in dark terracotta tiles. Stained glass, circular windows surrounded its façade.

'At Saint Dawn's Cathedral.'

Claude stared at it with apprehension. Abraham continued for a few feet, then stopped to inspect several trees.

'He's buried here, in the city?'

'Come lad, we are running out of time.' He ran his hands along a huge tree with a trunk several feet in circumference. There were no branches until at least ten feet up. Claude stood at the base of the tree with his axe and craned his head back to look up at it.

'This is impossible,' Claude said. 'I'll never get through it.'

'Well, Lad you said that about the first tree you cut down and you still did it. The more you stand there and complain about it, the more impossible it will seem,' he began to walk back towards the main path.

'Where are you going?'

'Bring the branch to the store when you are done. Make sure the twigs and leaves are removed but leave the rest intact.'

Claude watched him leave. The woodland suddenly became very silent. He looked at his wrinkled and pink hands. The first strike with the axe bounced off the tree like a rubber band. It reopened the old blisters and tore new skin off his palms and fingers. He stood looking up at the tree and slipped his shirt off. He wrapped it around the axe handle and tried again. A chip of wood flung over his shoulder as the axe sunk into the tree's torso.

Abraham stopped at the city gates and noticed several guards searching people's belongings as they entered. He also noticed he hadn't seen anyone leaving. He slid his hood on and tried to blend in with the farmers, but he was tall with a long, silver beard and would stand out no matter what he did. One of the guards nabbed him by his arm.

'You, stop,' the guard said, yanking him out of the crowd. As much as the guard tried, he could not pull Abraham off balance.

'What's your business in Shrub Oak?'

'And what business is it of yours?' Abraham responded, glaring at the guard. He held a long, iron pike with a rusted tip. His clothing and old armour were in shambles. He wore a pin on his breast plate that Abraham had not seen before. Another guard noticed the stall in the flow of people and rushed over.

'Is there a problem here?'

Abraham slowly and steadily slipped his hand into his cloak, reaching for his wand that was tucked into his belt.

'Let him through,' yelled a voice from high above them. All three looked up to see Ives Aries in the guard tower. He shouted at the guard lieutenant. 'I know this man. He is of no threat.'

Abraham looked at him with great scorn and pulled his arm away from the guard.

He continued on towards the store, noticing more and more guards stationed at every crossroads in the city. He took a detour away from his destination and headed towards Saint Dawn's cathedral. Outside was completely blocked by guards and priests trying to get in.

'Abraham!' yelped a man in a cassock of pure black. He was young and his hair was cut short.

'Brother Bishop,' Abraham said. 'What is going on here?'

'They came at night and made us all leave. We slept in the streets. Someone, a man, he wanted to search the cathedral. Now they won't let us back in.'

Abraham shook his head and lay his hand on

Brother Bishop's shoulder for comfort. 'He surely can't stop you from going in there for too much longer. Be patient, this will come to an end shortly.'

Brother Bishop nodded, looking back to his beloved home and sanctuary. Abraham hurried to his store. He took the back streets to avoid any further delays. As he rounded the corner, he realised he was in front of a freshly painted building with a large sign above it reading *Featherstone Antiquities*.

'Mr Crenshaw,' came a woman's voice from behind the plate-glass window. The door was pushed open and Mabel Featherstone came rushing out to greet him. 'Have you heard the news, Mr Crenshaw?'

He looked up to his store on the corner and could see two guards trying to hide in the shadows.

'News, Mrs Featherstone?'

'Well apparently there was an escaped convict roaming our streets, so the government has assigned more guards to keep watch. Scary, isn't it?'

Escaped convict? Abraham thought. *Ives Aries has put the town on lockdown while he searched for remains of Julius Oghast.*

'Yes,' Abraham finally said, finishing his thought. 'It's very scary indeed. I feel safer already.'

'Have you decided if you are coming to our grand opening? We have a guest of honour.'

'What? Oh, yes of course,' Abraham remembered. 'I would not miss it, now if you would excuse me, I am late to open my store.'

***

Claude looked up at the tree and cursed it for being so large. The breeze that carried through the ground smelled of sweet pine needles and fresh spring water. He had lent the axe on the tree and was sitting on an exposed boulder. His back was sore and ached wildly. His boots were full of woodchips and dried mud. His hands were curled into his palm, throbbing with agony. The heat had taken its toll and he had stumbled back, almost dropping the axe on his foot. He had thrown it a few feet, out of anger, then fetched it and lay it on the tree gently. He had no water, and no food. He lay back on the hard rock and was painfully uncomfortable but curled up the best he could and eventually fell asleep. He had the same dreams as he had that morning. He was standing beside his brother's grave, with his father's headstone beside it. His next vision was of his mother in their house. She was sitting in the dark, on a wooden chair and crying into her hands. He tried to talk to her, but she couldn't hear him. The house was dark and cold. He suddenly shot dead upright and nearly fell from the boulder he had been asleep on. Above him, the sun had moved across the sky and it was early afternoon. Claude was disappointed in himself for falling asleep and thought Abraham would be equally disappointed in him also. He picked up the axe and looked at the blade, as if to tell it to work with him, and not against him. Looking at his previous axe cuts, he could see they were haphazard and random, so he concentrated on one area. The axe sunk into the tree and carved a large chunk out and onto the ground at his feet. Several more hits in the same area and it started to moan and sway. He ignored the pain in his hands and yanked the axe out, then swung it back, burying it into the Gaboon Ebony tree. He hit it and hit it, one stroke after the other. Ignoring the pain. He could feel the tree about to give way, then from above, several birds took flight from the overgrown canopy. He looked up, seeing their wings spread wide as they flew east. Something had scared them. He looked deep into the woods surrounding him. There was only silence. Then came the agonizing scream from a man.

CHAPTER ELEVEN
MOONLESS NIGHT SKY

Claude unwrapped his shirt from the axe and slid it on. He stood looking into the darkness of the forest. Strips of fading light shown down from the holes in the foliage above. The scream had frightened him. His stomach was twisted, and his hands were shaking. He waited and listened as the forest became quiet once again. He stepped around the tree and could feel the presence of something far within the forest. After a few seconds, he turned back to the tree and kneeled down to pick the axe up, but suddenly froze in fear as a loud, ferocious growl came from behind him. Slowly, and apprehensively, he turned around. A giant bear was staring at him from the darkness. Its jowls were pulled back away from its gums, exposing its large, gnashing teeth. The animal stomped towards him, as if it was savouring each step so it could smell his fear. Claude was struck with utter terror. He felt the axe pull from his hands and drop to the ground. His knees and fingers started to shake. His mouth suddenly went dry and he couldn't blink his eyes.

'Shhh…' came from his mouth, as his brain tried to scare the animal away. 'Get out of here,' he managed to say while taking a step backward.

His heart was pounding so hard he thought it would leap out of his chest. The bear was massive. It was as tall as a human, but on four legs. Its fur was as brown and dark as the chestnuts he had seen on the ground in winter. Saliva dripped from its grating maw in long, jelly tendrils. It stood on its hind legs and let out an ear-piercing roar, shuddering through the forest, sending animals running for their lives. The massive bear launched onto its hindquarters and stepped forward, as if trained to walk on two legs. It arms out by its side. Long claws exposed and ready to slash.

A feeling of impending death hit his stomach and then legs. He was planted firmly onto the ground in terror. No matter what he told his brain, it wouldn't move. His eyes were wide and gleaming with tears. He closed his eyes, unable to watch the beast take its last few steps and devour him. He readied himself for impact. Then, from his right came the thunderous, booming, of footsteps. He opened one eye, just in time to see another huge bear bound through the thicket. It tore branches off trees and stones from the ground as if they were pebbles. It was covered in greying fur; its head and body were covered in scars and its black nose was as dark as a moonless night sky. Claude held his breath as the grey bear launched its body towards the brown bear, wrapping its huge arms around it and wrestling it to the ground. Claude didn't hesitate – he ran.

The broken twigs and branches tore at his clothes and boots. They cut his skin and snagged his hair. He didn't know which way he was going, but he knew the beasts were behind him, as he could hear them. Claude could almost feel their breath on the back of his neck. They made the most bestial noise he had ever heard. The clamping of teeth and the tearing of hair from skin amplified in the woodland. He ran without looking back. His back and arms started to throb with pain. He knew his feet were bleeding, but he didn't care. He suddenly reached a small threshold of shrubs and heard the sound of splashing water. Eagerly, he pushed his way through, still feeling his heart trying to tear from his chest. As he nudged through the small bank of shrubs, he came out into a small clearing. In front of him was a waterfall. He stared up at the massive wall of gushing water pouring out from somewhere unknown. It spat crystal clear liquid from a rocky and moss hewn mouth. He stood in open mouthed awe, letting the gentle spray of the water caress his face and body. His aching feet almost felt relieved.

A sound erupted from behind him, unlike any sound he had ever heard. A guttural moan, deep within somethings belly and reverberating off its diaphragm like two ships colliding on the sea. Claude snapped his head around as the brown bear flew through the undergrowth, slashing him across his chest in one mighty swing of its arm. His shirt, that had already been ruined by using it as an axe grip, sliced apart like warm butter. He felt the claws, razor sharp, cut his skin and he fell backwards. As he landed on the muddy bank. The wet soil was a soft cushion for his beaten and bloodied body. He looked up at the sky already accepting what was about to happen to him. The, eclipsing the sun, was the grey bear. It appeared atop a jagged stone ledge protruding from the waterfall. It growled, ready to pounce.

Claude's eyes tried to focus, but his injuries were making everything turn fuzzy. It leapt from the stony outcropping and landed right by Claude's head, rushing towards the brown bear. It bit into the bear's shoulder, then kicked it backwards. The grey bear turned back to Claude. It was so fast he hardly got to register the bear had moved. It grabbed him by the arm and lifted him up, tossing him into the water. Claude flew through the air and landed with a splash. He felt water envelope his body but stopped just short of his bleeding chest. He was laying against the fall as water streamed down onto his face. Through the watery curtain, and his blurred vision, he saw the two bears fight, then everything started to fade to black. The water was cooling, but his wounds were too painful and soon the darkness took him.

'Lad!' came a voice, shouting over the raging water. 'Claude!' He recognised the voice of Abraham.

'Here!' he shouted, muggy in his own voice.

'Lad! We have to get you help!' Abraham's voice was in a panic.

'No,' Claude said, feeling Abrahams arms under him and then picking him up. 'I'm okay.'

He took him out of the water and laid him down on the soft ground.

'You scared me half to death,' Abraham said, his voice shaking. 'I came back to fetch you and you were gone.'

'A bear came out of the woods…' Claude mustered with struggled breath.

'A bear? You got into the middle of a bear fight, lad? You're lucky to be alive!'

'No,' Claude said, sitting up. 'One saved me… it threw me in the water.'

Abraham looked behind Claude, at the waterfall. He was some distance away from the bear prints on the ground.

'Never mind that lad, we have to get you back home.'

'But the tree…' Claude said, as he felt his body being picked up again, and he slowly drifted off into unconsciousness.

When Claude woke, he was laying across Abrahams chair with a knitted, woollen, blanket over his legs. The cat Oka, was curled up on his lap, gently purring. He slowly looked around the room to get his bearings and saw a large pot over a stove. It was bubbling with a ladle poking out of it. It smelt divine. The fireplace was freshly stacked with wood and it crackled and burped embers up into the chimney chute.

'You gave me quite a fright there, lad,' said Abrahams' voice from the hallway. He entered the room wearing long johns, his boots and a ragged white shirt with some blood on it.

'Bears scare me more than anything,' Claude said, moving his gaze back to the cat and patting it softly.

'They should,' Abraham stated. 'They're a terrifying beast, capable of taking out ten men. A small lad like you, would be no problem.'

'One killed my brother,' Claude said, looking up at Abraham's back, as he stirred the pot. Abraham suddenly stopped moving. He was frozen with thought. 'He got lost in the woods and I went to find him…'

'Rest, Claude.'

'Maybe one of them is the one that killed by brother? I should go back there and…'

'Get yourself killed, lad?' Abraham said, his voice was loud and commanding. He marched a bowl of broth over to Claude. 'Enough of this talk. You're covered in bruises and scratches. Eat up. This will fix you and heal the stitches.'

Claude looked down at his chest. He hadn't noticed the throbbing pain. His entire chest was wrapped in gauze. Strips of white cloth criss-crossed his ribcage, with very little blood seeping through.

'Stitches?'

'The bear got you along the chest, right on your sternum. Three claw marks. If they were any deeper, you may not be sipping that soup right now. Two of the scratches were not deep enough for stitches. I cleaned them the best I could. One scratch was deep. I used three stitches in the middle, that is all.'

'How did I get back here?'

'I carried you.'

Oka stood up and stretched its long legs and leapt down to the rug on the floor.

'You carried me all the way back? What about the branch?'

'It's at the back of the house. Shaved of its twigs, ready for the lathe,' he sat down at the table and tore the end off a fresh loaf of bread, then dipped it into the stew.

'How did you…?'

'Never mind that lad, eat your stew and rest. I need your help tomorrow.'

They ate in silence.

CHAPTER TWELVE
PETRIFIED

Every time Claude cranked the wheel for the lathe, his stitches pulled and sent a sharp pain up his shoulder. He wasn't entirely sure he should have been turning the wheel, but Abraham was insistent and needed to get the wand finished. They had walked to the store in the rain again, saying very little. The sombre mood, Claude assumed, was due to the man he called Ives Aries and the black wand he required. Abraham seemed to stare off into the distance, as if contemplating the future.

As soon as the store was open, he ordered Claude to turn the wheel until the branch was resembling a wand. The shavings were piled up at his feet like mole hills. The muscles in his shoulders and forearms stung and throbbed with every turn. Claude was determined not to show how much pain he was in, as he knew how important this task was.

'Stop, lad,' Abraham said, his own hands hurting from holding the metal file.

Abraham sat wearing his long denim apron. Filed pieces of wood covered his front and down onto the floor and onto the torn and ratty rug under the lathe. No one had come into the store for the last hour, but in the morning, there had been several people looking to buy furnishings which pushed them further behind schedule. Abraham looked at his swollen knuckles and tried desperately to shake the pain away.

'I want you to go to the deli and buy us some more bread and several slices of smoked ham. It's in the middle of town, Old Samson's. You won't get lost. It's at the end of the road we are on.' He got up and went to the cash register, fetching several coins and placing them in Claude's hand. 'Don't be too long.' Claude nodded and took the money.

The breeze outside was welcoming on his face. He let his arms dangle beside him, relieved to have stopped turning the wheel for a moment. He wandered up the cobblestone road to the corner where Featherstone Antiquities store was busy with people shuffling in and out. The door was pushed open as Avery shoved her way outside, screaming something to her mother as she left.

'Claude?' she said, surprised to see him.

'Avery,' Claude said, not knowing if to bow or do something else.

'Where are you off to?'

'I'm going to get us provisions for lunch.'

'May I walk with you?'

Claude nodded. The city was bustling with people, even more so then the first day he had seen it. The guards kept people moving and wouldn't allow them to loiter for longer than a minute.

'So, is Abraham your father or just employer?' she asked, looking at him with a sideways glance.

'I am his apprentice. I've only known him for

several days. I'm from Yorktown and don't know anyone here,' Claude said, feeling a kinship towards Abraham already.

'Good thing I came along then,' she said, with a smile, as they crossed the street. A long line of horse drawn carts were lined up along one side, feeding from their bags.

'Why is that?'

'Someone your own age. No offence, but Mr Crenshaw looks as old as my mother. All they want to do is work, work, work.'

Claude never thought about making friends with anyone. The only friend he really had back home was his brother, and he worked because his father couldn't.

'Look at that strange man,' Avery said, pointing to a man in religious attire. He was walking around hunched over like an animal. Most people walking through the city centre were either avoiding him or paying him no attention.

The man leapt into the air and started to sniff the ground. He ran his hands along the long pieces of stone, flatted by years of horse hooves and heavy carriages. Suddenly, he stood up, as if some spell had been broken and began to look around very confused.

'What do you think he's doing?' Claude said, still gripping the money Abraham gave him tightly.

'Let's see where he goes,' Avery said, crouching down and following him.

Claude looked around the centre he had found

himself in and noticed the deli was behind him. He had walked right past it. 'I really need to get back…' he said, but Avery was gone. 'Avery?'

His arm was snatched, and he was dragged through the streets by the small girl. They rushed into an alleyway and hid.

'I'm not sure…'

'Hush, Claude,' Avery demanded, briefly glancing around the corner. 'He's heading into the cathedral.'

Claude suddenly found it very hard to swallow. He popped his head out of the alleyway and could see the man had paused at the doors of Saint Dawn's Cathedral. The two front handles were chained together. His heart sunk into his stomach as a feeling of dread passed over him.

'We gotta go,' he said abruptly, rushing out of the alleyway and straight into a man standing so still he could have been a statue. 'I'm so very sorry,' Claude said, looking up as the man turned around. Ives Aries looked down at him, and grinned.

'Well, if it isn't the apprentice boy.'

'I'm sorry, Sir. I really must be on my way.'

'Why are you in such a hurry?' Ives said, gripping Claude's shoulder. His stitches started to pull tight. Avery tried to step in between them, she shoved her body so close to Claude's that Ives had to step back. He eyed the girl with contempt.

'Tell your master that my… merchandise better be ready by tomorrow morning.' Ives stared at Claude, as if trying to stare right into his very thoughts.

Avery pulled Claude away as he kept his gaze upon him. They made a quick detour to the deli and picked up the provisions, then headed back to the store. There were less people now on the streets as the day started to fade into early evening.

'I get a bad feeling about that man,' Avery said, as they approached the Featherstone Antiquities storefront. 'He comes by to see my mother every day we've been here. He's ordered a lot of stuff from us.'

'Like what?'

'If you are coming to the grand opening party tonight, I'll show you,' she said, giving him a smile and running back inside her mother's store. Claude stood in the street holding bread and a package of cured meat. He then ran his hand over his chest, feeling the crossed stitchwork on his skin. He had momentarily forgotten about it.

As he entered the store, he noticed the lamp by the front desk was out. The entire room was in darkness.

'Abraham?' Claude said softly as he stepped through the maze of cabinets and dressers, the bread in one hand and the wrapped meat in newspaper in the other. A hand from the darkness reached out, bony and leathery. It gripped his hand and Claude shrieked, leaping into the air, dropping the bread.

'Calm yourself boy, it's only me,' said Agnes the witch. 'We've been waiting for you.'

Abraham heard the commotion from the woodworking room. He tried to lift the lathe, but his bones felt like they were on fire. He looked up to see

Agnes hobbling down the stairs, followed by a petrified Claude.

'What took you so long, lad, we'd half starve to death if you took any longer.'

'The cathedral,' Claude managed to say, placing the bread and meat on the counter.

'What about it?'

Claude looked from Agnes to Abraham, then back to Agnes. 'It's chained up. I saw a priest, he looked lost. He was trying to get in, but… that man, Ives, was there, watching him from an alleyway.'

Agnes slowly turned towards Abraham. Her eyes were narrowed. 'He's found it.'

Abraham nodded his head. 'Lad, help me move the lathe.'

Claude was still amazed of the tasks being asked of him. He had been attacked by a bear and flung several feet into a waterfall only the evening before last, and he was still being asked to cut trees and move lathes.

'Why are we moving it?' he questioned.

Abraham didn't answer. He lifted one end and grimaced. Claude lifted the other end and they slid it off the rug. When Claude looked back to Agnes, she was holding a thin piece of cylindrical wood in her hand. It was carved delicately, wrapped in soft velvet and had several small bones attached to the handle by string.

'Is that the…wand?' Claude said.

'Claude!' Abraham shouted, frustrated. 'Ask questions later, help me with the rug.'

Abraham yanked the rug, but it was so heavy with fallen debris that it took two people to roll up. Underneath the rug, was a square door with a round, iron handle. He bent down and jerked the handle up. The door flung open, coughing up a cloud of dust. Several steps led down into a dark abyss. Claude was too afraid to ask what was down there.

Agnes marched down first, followed by Abraham. 'Claude, turn the closed sign on the door and lock it,' Abraham said before disappearing down into the dark. He gave him a look that was both embarrassed that he had snapped and anxious.

Claude ran through the store and pulled the curtains across the windows. He slid the deadbolt across the door and turned the sign over. The afternoon light outside was now blocked by the thick, velvet curtains. The showroom was cast in shadowy darkness. He ran back to the trap door and noticed a glow of light being cast up the staircase. Steadily, he made his way down. The timber beams were covered in cobwebs and strands of dust. The dangling threads of dirt and old webs swayed in an overdraft coming from the rear door. The bottom of the stairs were roughly laid stones. As he reached the bottom, he saw the room was vast, completely wall to wall with shelves, draws, old termite eaten cupboards and hundreds of small, rectangular boxes. Wands were displayed in glass cases, each one with a silver plaque. The ground was bare except where Abraham and Agnes were standing. Abraham stood back near a table with several parchments of paper lay. They were scribbled with red diagrams. Several candles were burning around the room. The basement smelt of rosemary and thyme, burning vanilla candles and old treatment oil. On the ground, at Agnes's feet, a triangle pattern had been drawn in what appeared to be burnt ash. In the middle of the triangle, was the black wand.

'Stand back, lad,' Abraham said, reaching for the parchments and handing them to Agnes. 'And cover your face.'

Claude took several steps back, as instructed. On the bench behind him was a taxidermied head of an animal he had never seen in his life. It had long ears and curled fangs growing over its bottom jaw. There were several jars of eyes and even one jar containing a gnarled hoof. Agnes started to read from the scripture. She hummed and waved her hands delicately in the air, as if orchestrating a choir. Her long hair peeled away from her face, revealing her skin to be wrinkled and distraught. Suddenly, the wand shot upwards into the air, bouncing off the ceiling and rocketing towards Claude. He ducked just in time as it ricocheted off a jar and bounced off a glass cabinet near Abraham. Finally, after zooming around the room uncontrollably, it landed back inside the triangle as Agnes read the last sentence. Claude, who had been covering his eyes, gingerly looked through his fingers at the wand. It popped like cooking popcorn, then rolled around, as if sizzling on a hotplate. Agnes bent down and picked it up. The wood stretched and sounded like it was about to splinter.

'It's equipped with the spell and nothing else. After it is used, it will break. Ives will not be able to use it further,' she picked it up and studied it.

Abraham took it carefully from the witch and together, they marched back upstairs. They threw the rug back over the trap door and moved the lathe over it. Abraham slipped it into a silk lined box and tied a black ribbon around it. He carefully placed it on a dusty mantle in the woodwork room.

'Ives will collect it in the morning for the ritual the following night, is my guess,' Agnes stated, gathering her belongings. She slipped on a long black cloak with red stitching down the arms. Several brooches were attached to the left side.

'We will wait till tomorrow night and break into the cathedral, making sure Julius Oghast does not rise again.'

'Sleep well,' Agnes said, pushing the rear door open and sliding into the blue hue of night.

'The grand opening of Featherstone Antiquities is tonight,' Claude said.

'We will go for a short time, then head home. Making our presence known at an event will distance us from what is happening around the city and cathedral.'

'Is that something we need to worry about?' Claude asked.

'With Ives Aries bringing in more guards, he will

not want us around if he suspects we have found out what he is doing. It's best we are seen.'

Claude understood.

CHAPTER THIRTEEN
THE LIGHT OF THE LANTERN

Abraham had made Claude wash his face and clean his boots. Claude was given a neckerchief to tie around his neck. It was bright blue. The knot sat over his stitches, with the two ends hanging down his front. Abraham inspected his young apprentice and patted his shoulder. His face dropped into concern.

'Something wrong?' Claude said.

'No, lad. Nothing is wrong,' Abraham said.

Claude knew he was lying, but he didn't want to ask. Abraham had found an old, long-coat in his office which he tried to scrub clean. It was too far to walk home to change and get back in time. Abraham cleaned his shoes the best he could, covering the scuff marks with boot oil. He combed his beard and wore his own neckerchief around his neck, it was the same colour as Claude's. They walked outside and Abraham locked the door behind them. The air was crisp and fresh, making Claude pull his neckerchief higher up under his chin. The streets were still full of people scurrying around getting their last-minute shopping or attending the local taverns. As they made their way down to the Antique store, Claude noticed a long queue of people waiting for their chance to enter the store. The thoroughfare nearly ran the length of the street.

'Quite a reception,' Abraham noted.

'All this for antiquities?' Claude questioned, looking at the people dressed in their best attire.

'They aren't just antiquities, lad. The import of goods is new to this area. It's expanding the city, bringing in more people,' Abraham said, heading to the end of the line.

The air was chilly, giving hints of autumn.

'Why would it bring in more people?'

'Stores like this, and even my store, aren't common, lad. To build a town, you need a provision store and a tavern. To build a city, you need money. Places like this give them a chance to spend their money. Something of high value.'

'Is that why Ives Aries has ordered antiquities from Mrs Featherstone?'

Abraham turned to him. 'Who told you that?'

'Avery told me today,' Claude said matter-of-factly.

Someone stepped out of the massive building, waving their hands and hollering.

'Mr Crenshaw!' Mabel yelped over the crowd.

Claude stepped out from behind Abraham and saw Mabel heading towards them, her eyes beaming. She wore a decadent dress with white tassels and meticulously detailed floral patterns running down both sleeves. She took Abraham by his head and dragged him from the line.

'Hurry, Claude,' Mabel said, marching back to the store front where two men in red suits held the door open for her. 'Avery is bored out of her mind. She's been waiting for you.'

As they were dragged through the door, Abraham lent down to Claude, 'Keep your eyes peeled. If you see anyone acting suspicious, come and get me.'

Claude looked around noting all the people gathered around large pieces of obscure antiques and vintage oddities. The people looked well dressed, with expensive jewellery and their noses in the air. Abraham was pulled away by Mabel. She took him to a small gathering of people standing around a large, finely painted, vase. Claude was suddenly left on his own. A waiter walked past wearing white cloves and offered him a tall glass of water with several pieces of fruit floating in it. As he reached for it, someone rushed through the crowd and took his hand, making him spill some of his water on the ground.

'Don't drink that,' Avery said, wearing the exact same dress as her mother. She led him through the room, which was larger than any establishment he had ever been in. It appeared to go further back.

'Why can't I drink it?'

'It's fruit imported from who knows where. It's been on a ship for two months.'

Claude put his drink on the next table they passed. Right when he thought they had reached the end, there was another room, with more eccentric objects.

'Where are you taking me?' Claude demanded to know.

'I gotta show you something.'

They squeezed through a group of people who looked down at them with revulsion. Avery seemed to ignore them as they approached a large table towards the rear of the room. It was decorated eloquently with fine embroideries and polished cutlery. The table was covered in food that made Claude freeze. Pastries, cake and small pieces of cucumber and cheese were laid out before him. Avery dropped to her knees and disappeared under the table. Claude stood there for a moment, trying to figure out what was going on. From under the tablecloth, a hand appeared and yanked him under.

'Follow me,' Avery said, crawling through to the other side.

Claude followed her under the table. On the other side, a large sheet had been pulled across making a make-shift wall between the showroom and the back office.

'Where are we?'

'Just the storage area,' she replied, fumbling in the dark for a lantern. The flickering of light filled the glass chimney of the lamp. Avery's face was splashed with the yellow light. Her hair cascaded down her face, and the soft illumination embellished her deep green eyes. 'It's back here.'

The shuffling sound of feet and the chattering from the main room started to die away as Claude was led through a long hallway filled with wooden boxes and parcels, stacked to the ceiling. At the end of the hallway was a door. It looked brand new, with polished silver hinges. Avery gave Claude the lantern and dug in her dress, pulling out a key. Claude looked behind them but couldn't hear anyone coming their way.

'What's in here?' he asked, turning back as Avery opened the door.

The door swung open revealing a room that was packed to the trusses with large boxes. All of them were marked with postage stamps and bizarre inscriptions, they still smelled like the sea from their long journeys. Claude stuck the lantern out in front of him as he watched Avery disappear into the labyrinth of crates. The lantern dimmed and sent light dancing around the room.

'Avery?' Claude said, nervousness in his voice. In the dark, he couldn't tell which way she went.

'Back here,' came the voice from the dark.

Unexpectedly, the room was cast in a bright blue glow. It overpowered the light of the lantern and lit the room up in spectacular rays of indigo. Claude placed the lantern on the ground as he saw Avery coming towards him with an open box, it was the source of the beaming light. Inside it, was a long-handled blade.

'What is that?' Claude asked, staring with hypnotic awe.

'Mother ordered it in for Mr Aries. I saw it glowing blue when I came into fetch the ledger scrolls Mum had left in here. It doesn't glow all the time,' she said, reaching for it.

'Don't touch it,' Claude warned. Her hand paused a few inches from the handle.

'It's okay,' she replied, looking up at him. 'Bring the lantern here, I'll show you something else.'

Claude fetched the lantern and held it high. Avery gently picked up the long blade. Its blue aura was mesmerising. It gave off a feeling of warmth and splendour. She held it to the small flame inside the lantern. A howl tore through the small room as its radiant hue was snuffed out in an instant.

'It went out?'

'When I was helping mother unpack it, I held it up to a small torch to look at the inscriptions, and the flame leapt out and licked it. The handle went so cold I dropped it.'

'What does it mean?' Claude said.

From behind the velvet curtain came the pounding of heavy boots.

'Quick, hide!' Avery said, slamming the knife back in the box.

Claude spun around in a circle, suddenly panicked. Avery grabbed him by the hand and led him deeper into the maze of crates. She grabbed the lantern and blew out the flame. The bootsteps stopped at the door, then it paused for a moment, as if examining the room. Then the door creaked open and the pounding boots continued. Whoever it was, walked in gently and stopped short of where they had been standing only a moment ago. Claude knelt on the ground with Avery in front of him, holding the box. Emerald green light started to emanate from the lid. Avery looked down at it in surprise, trying to cover it with her dress. Claude snatched it as the unknown figure made its way towards them. He hid it under his coat. From down the hall came the clanging of glasses and they could hear Mabel Featherstone call everyone to attention. The figure turned around sharply, grunted and headed back towards the door, slamming it shut as they went.

'That was close,' Claude said, sliding the blade box out from his coat.

Avery placed the blade back where she had found it and together, they ran back down the hallway, clambered under the table and re-joined the party just as Mabel was stepping upon a make-shift stage constructed from empty crates.

'Attention please!' she demanded. 'First of all, I would just like to thank everyone for coming tonight. It's been a rough journey to get this far, but we believe that Featherstone Antiquities has finally found their home here in Shrub Oak.' A round of applause followed. 'When the previous store burnt down…' there was a pause as Mabel choked back emotions at the very thought of the memory, 'we were determined to reopen it, better than before with products being shipped from all over the world.'

Claude saw a lone figure cutting through the crowd, heading toward the stage. It was Ives Aries. He was wearing a suit with bright silver buttons and large, heavy, black boots. He scanned the crowd, as if looking for someone. Abraham had his back against the far wall. Claude could see his line of sight was directly on Ives.

'We look forward to many years of business here, as we now call this place home.' Another round of applause as Mabel lifted her glass into the air. 'Thank you all. Now, I would like to invite a special guest up to the podium, a man that needs no introduction, a man who, without him, this would not have been possible due to his generous business, Mr Ives Aries.'

Claude looked at Avery, who was equally stunned.

'Thank you, Mrs Featherstone, a delight to be here,' he started, watching as Mabel left the stage and stood beside Abraham. He stepped on stage and looked out at the crowd gathered. 'With newer and improved ships and roads, trading routes and wagons, it has paved a new, safer, way to import goods... and services. Stores like this are our connection to the rest of the world. Where once we would only dream of obtaining certain objects, now, we can get them shipped in a matter of days.'

Abraham lent over to Mabel and whispered, 'I don't trust him.'

Mabel turned her head slightly to meet his gaze, 'He has provided me with a huge down payment on articles from overseas... He allowed me to open the shop. He may seem that way, but once you speak to him...' her sentence was cut short as Ives started to raise his voice over the murmur.

'This event is the perfect time to announce that I

will be moving permanently to Shrub Oak. My operations across the sea will be rehoused here and I hope to become the first Count of Shrub Oak.' He raised his glass. 'In honour of future endeavours and may it bring us good fortune.'

The crowd erupted in applause. The audience gathered around the stage slowly dispersed. Ives stepped down and headed straight to Mabel and Abraham.

'Mrs Featherstone, thank you for the opportunity to be the guest of honour tonight,' Ives said, moving his steel gaze to Abraham.

'I had no idea that you were planning on becoming the Count of Shrub Oak,' Mabel said, confused.

'The city is growing, Mrs Featherstone. The lands are for sale and the city guards and lawmakers are inundated… I plan on growing it further, revitalising the economy and bringing business into the county. A gesture the people of Shrub Oak will surely embrace.'

'I wouldn't be so sure,' Abraham said.

The two men were nearly equal in height. Ives appeared to brood over Abrahams comment, as if he wanted to retaliate, but held it back. His deep black hair was combed back, his face was cleanly shaved, and his sunken cheekbones displayed deep shadows. He had a cut on his neck that disappeared down his collar.

'And why is that, Mr….'

Mabel stood between them, her hand raised. 'If you would excuse me, I really must introduce Mr Aries to another client of mine.'

Abraham kept his eyes locked on Ives as he turned away and faded into the crowd with Mabel. Quickly, he searched through the crowd until he found Claude. He was sitting with Avery, eating small sandwiches.

'Come, boy, we are going.'

Claude put his plate on the table and waved goodbye to Avery. They walked out into the night air. It was cold and dreary. The soft fog that had come through the city hid the cobblestones in a thick blanket of white. The moon was partially disguised by several darkening clouds.

They strolled back down the street, pulling their coats tightly around their necks and fastening their neckerchiefs. Abraham suddenly stopped; his body froze. Claude looked at him, then followed his line of sight. The front door to their store was open. Shrapnel's of wood and metal lay on the steps. The door was nearly ripped from its hinges. Abraham reached into his cloak and pulled out a wand.

'Stay here lad,' he said, entering the darkened store.

CHAPTER FOURTEEN
THREE CATS

Claude stood in the dark street outside the store. Lanterns were lit along the cobblestone roads, bolted atop lengths of wood. The light it supplied was dull and barely lit the street. The fog crawled around his feet and sent chills up his legs and spine. Abraham had been gone for some time, and he hadn't heard anything from inside. Claude stepped up to the front door and peered in. The drawers and shelving units had been all pushed apart haphazardly, leaving the showroom in disarray. Claude tentatively stepped into the doorway.

'Abraham?' he said, at half a whisper.

The only answer he heard came from the howling wind outside. The streetlights flickered against the windowpanes. He cautiously stepped toward the counter. The lantern that normally sat beside the ledger was missing. Claude went around the counter and down into the small office at the rear. Abrahams scrolls were scattered over the floor. Several half-finished wands were broken in half and tossed carelessly against the wall. Claude bent down to pick them up. He had helped to turn the wheel for most of them and was sad to see them destroyed. The sound of clanging metal came from his right. He snapped his head to the source of the sound and saw the door to the woodwork room slowly peel open.

'Abraham?'

Glancing in, he could see the lathe was pushed on its side, pieces of it were broken off. The rug had been kicked into a corner. Multiple boxes from the towering shelving units had been tossed to the ground. They had been opened and either torn open or ripped apart. The stairs leading down to the basement were dark. Claude could see the first step, then it was swallowed in obscurity.

'Abraham?' he said down the stairwell.

'Down here, lad,' came a sullen voice.

Claude knew something was wrong. He had never heard his master's voice sound that crestfallen. A small flicker of light lit the staircase and Claude could hear Abraham slowly make his way up to the woodwork floor.

'They've taken the wand.'

'Who has?'

'I assume Ives Aries,' Abraham said, throwing his coat into the mess and slipping his neckerchief off. He dug through the rubble and found his long, black, hooded cloak and put it on.

'But we were with him all night?' Claude answered.

'Then it was one of the guards!' Abraham spat, losing his temper. 'Come, lad, we must find it before they either give it to Ives or use it.'

They rushed out of the store, leaving the front door off its hinges. The fog was thicker now that it was later in the night. The streetlamps were dimming from running out of oil or from being strangled by the mist. Abraham walked as if he knew where he was going, and Claude followed. They marched up the street, avoiding the main roads where the guards were stationed.

'Where are we going?'

'The cathedral, lad. Ives must have lied about when he needed the wand by. They must be performing the resurrection of the Arch Mage tonight.'

Ahead of them, in the smoky alleyway was a figure moaning and walking with a prolific stagger. Abraham stopped for a moment, looking at the silhouette of the figure as he fell to the ground, into the garbage and picked himself up again.

'That looks like… Brother Bishop?' Abraham said.

He entered the alley way with trepid footfalls. The garbage and discarded paper under them crunched loudly, making Brother Bishop spin around, as if some invisible hand twirled him on a spinning top. In his left hand, he brandished the black wand.

'Brother Bishop,' Abraham said softly. 'It's me, Abraham Crenshaw.'

The clergyman cocked his head to one side and stepped into the glow of a streetlight. His eyes were pure white, void of pupils and cornea. His steps were timid and clumsy.

'Put it down, Brother Bishop… please,' Abraham pleaded. He raised his hand to take it, but Brother Bishop launched at him, his teeth gnarled.

Abraham pushed Claude to the side and took the full impact of the possessed man. His arms flayed about like a mad sea creature taking down a ship. Abraham's wand was knocked out of his hand and landed at Claude's feet. Abraham tried to push him off, but Brother Bishop had a strong hold on him. They scuffled and Abraham hit him in the chest and stomach, but the man didn't seem to react to it. Claude snatched the wand and held it to the sky, he closed his eyes and felt a sleeping energy awaken in him. It traversed through his body like electricity and surged up his arms into the wand, as if it was part of his body. The tip of the wand lit up in a bright, lime green flame. He didn't know what was happening, but he found himself pointing the want at the wrestling men. He waited for his opportune moment. Abraham kicked Brother Bishop off him, and Claude watched as the energy blast snaked from the wand. It soared through the air, hitting Brother Bishop and sending him back several feet against the brick wall. From behind Claude came the sound of many feet running. As he turned, he was stuck in the back by something and collapsed forward, the wand torn from his hand by a masked man with searing green eyes. He opened one eye to see the wand being stomped on, snapping it into several pieces. The alleyway was suddenly filled with movement and chaos.

'Claude!' he could hear Abraham call in the darkness. His vision was starting to fade. 'Run!'

Claude forced his eyes open, and the darkness

retreated from his mind. He got to his feet with the aid of the wall. His legs were still wobbly. Several people in metallic masks with emerald green eyes were dragging Abraham toward the far end of the alley. His hands were trying to grip the ground. Claude could see the fear in his face.

'Run!' Abraham shouted at him, as his voice was suddenly muffled.

Claude did what he had been doing his whole life, he ran.

When his father got sick and he was ordered to fetch the Doctor, he ran. When they ran out of food and clean water, he ran. When his mother lay on the bed for days, not moving, he ran. He ran to get away.

The streets were a catacomb of flickering lanterns and never-ending cobblestone thoroughfares. The inky blackness was like a thick blanket, sitting over the city. The white fog beneath it, clouding the streets bumpy and uneven terrain. It climbed up the light-poles and lingered along the brick walls. Claude ran out up the street to the cathedral where he could see several lights coming from the windows. He kept running until he got lost, then continued running more. His calves pulled and strained. His boots started to fall apart, pieces flying off as they caught on the brick and stone. He followed the streets through the housing district and further into farmland where he was met with the wall that surrounded Shrub Oak. He stared at it, as if waiting for it to move. Then he continued running beside it, through muddy grasslands, over hills and through a cow field. His mind was racing as fast as his feet were. Finally, he re-entered the city limits and saw the gate to the city. Several guards were sleeping at their posts, their helmets drawn down over their eyes. He ran straight past them without waking them. He sprinted down the long and winding path back to Abraham's home.

He suddenly came to the realisation that he didn't have a key. He stared at the door, racking his brain for a solution. He pressed on the door, and jiggled the handle, but it was no use. He stepped back a few steps and looked up at the next level. His window was open slightly. A habit he had gotten into when he lived at home. He levered himself up the windowsill, grabbing the edge of the roof. His hand slipped and he fell back onto the ground. He stood up, taking a deep breath. He took a few steps back and ran towards the side window, stomping on some of Abraham's plants as he leapt into the air. His fingers gripped the ledge. As they started to slip, he kicked his feet, pushing off the windowsill, and used the motion to swing his right leg onto the roof edge. Claude struggled to pull himself up, but noticed his arms were stronger than he remembered. He scampered across the brittle roof. Underneath his feet, he could hear the hatch starting to crack. Slowly, he stepped towards his window and slid it open. Sweat was running down his neck as he stepped into his room and onto his mattress. He collapsed onto his bed, finally able to rest for a moment. His heart pumped erratically. Given it was cold outside, sweat still beaded on his brow. The house was dark and still. His heartbeat was in his ears and his lungs felt like they wanted to press through his ribcage. He lay there for several moments, thinking of what had just happened. Someone had taken Abraham, and he knew it had to be Ives Aries.

Get help, came a voice.

Claude shot up, looking around. It didn't sound like a person's voice. It sounded like a distant memory, speaking to him inside his head.

'Who's there?' he asked the darkness. His bedroom door was open.

A pure black cat strolled in from the hallway and stopped just short of Claude. It licked its paws and then proceeded to clean its ears.

'You must be one of Abraham's other cats,' Claude said to it. From behind the black cat, came the ginger cat.

Where's Abraham? said another voice.

Claude reacted by leaping to his feet and backing away from the cats, pushing his back against the wall. A third cat came in from the depths of the house. It was pure white and sat in the dark, staring at Claude.

'Abraham was taken… I think by a man called Ives Aries,' Claude said, feeling a little silly for talking to three cats.

The pure white cat stepped forward and sat by Claude's feet and looked up at him.

Get help, came the same voice as before. Claude

shook his head. He thought he must be going mad. He leapt onto his bed, sliding the window back open and jumped out. His foot went halfway through the roof. He yanked it out, slid down the rest of the thatched roof and dropped onto the ground and started running.

CHAPTER FIFTEEN
SAINT SEBASTIAN

The knocks were loud, and Claude could hear it echoing up the belfry and making the bell hum. He stood back and looked at the church. It was nearly the middle of the night and the surrounding church yard was hidden in the fog. It hung around the gravestones like suspended cotton wool. He lifted his fists again and bashed harder on the door. He tried the handle, but it was locked. Suddenly, from deep inside the church, he could hear footsteps running towards him. The door swung open, nearly knocking him off the first step. Father Jacob looked around frantically, fumbling with his glasses.

'Who's that? Who's there?' His head bobbed about like a fishing float in the water.

'Father Jacob, it's me, Claude!'

'Claude Wells? What are you doing here at this time of night? Is there something wrong with your father?'

He was so close to home, that the thought had crossed his mind to sneak in quickly. But it would worry his parents if they knew his master had been kidnapped.

'No, it's Mr Crenshaw.'

Father Jacob looked around the front yard of the church, expecting to see him.

'Where is he?'

'He's been taken.'

Father Jacob swung around, his night-gown fanning out behind him as he ran back into the church. Claude stepped back up the stairs and went inside. He saw Father Jacob rushing through the pews and passed the podium to the rectory at the rear of the building. Claude was unsure what was happening. The church was dark and cold. He could hear Father Jacob muttering and moving around frantically.

'Where did they take him?' he shouted from the back room.

'I...' Claude paused for a moment. He thought about what he was about to say, and he knew it was going to sound strange, 'they took him to the cathedral in Shrub Oak. An old Mage is buried there, Julius Oghast. Ives Aries needed a black wand to raise him from the dead.'

Father Jacob came out of the room and paused. His jaw was open, and his eyes were nearly popping out of his head.

'They have a black wand?' Father Jacob said surprised, slipping his boots on. 'If this is all correct, then we have no time, we must hurry.'

Claude was quite surprised how Father Jacob had taken the information.

'How did you...?'

'Time is of the essence! We must hurry. Questions can be for later!'

Claude followed him out the front door and

around the side of the church. The ground was slippery with mildew. He could feel its cold touch through the holes in his shoes.

'Where are you going?' Claude said, frustrated. 'The city is this way.'

'We have no time, Claude Wells. We need to take the horse.'

At the rear of the church was a small, dilapidated, outhouse, and beside it a two-stable barn. The barn housed one horse, as far as Claude could see in the dark and not much else. Father Jacob pulled the horse out and Claude got to see it in the moonlight. It looked older than the church itself, and the church was very old. Its mane was mattered and grey, and its eyes were deep black and ringed with purple, fleshy bags. A small, two-person, carriage was attached to the horse in a matter of minutes. Father Jacob flapped about, clipping together buckles and straps. Claude was growing more and more inpatient. Swiftly, Father Jacob launched himself onto the wagon.

'Get on, Claude Wells! We must get going!' Claude climbed on quickly. The bench seat was attached to springs that pushed through the torn leather seat. 'This wagon belonged to the first parishioner here,' he said, looking at Claude. 'It's never been replaced, not once, and it's good as new. And that is the same with this horse, Saint Sebastian.'

Claude didn't agree that the wagon was like new, however, when Father Jacob clicked his fingers, Saint Sebastian bolted faster than any horse he had ever seen in his life. The fog parted as the horse pounded its hooves across the ground. Soon, they were out of Yorktown's outer rim and into the long winding road to Shrub Oak.

As the wind tore at his hair and clothes, Claude managed to hold on for dear life. He turned towards Father Jacob. He was the man that spoke at his brother's funeral. He had come to visit his father when he became ill and performed a service at his bedside.

'How do you know about Ives Aries?' Claude asked, as the speed they were going made it difficult to hear.

'The heritage of this town goes very far back, Claude Wells,' he said, driving the stirrups hard against the leather bar. 'A new magical awakening is occurring, and we are at the forefront of this insurgence. Ives Aries has attempted to come to this land many times before, but he was always stopped by the Bacre Keep wizards.'

'He's here now, though.'

'Which puts fear in my belly, Claude Wells. If Ives Aries is here, what happened to the wizards?'

Father Jacob remained quiet for the rest of the journey until they reached the gates of Shrub Oak. As they approached the walls, Claude noticed the guards were lying on the ground. At first glance, he thought they were sleeping. Father Jacob pulled the cart alongside them and brought it to a halt. He leapt off and checked their pulse, they had perished by longswords.

'Hop down, Claude Wells. We will walk from here. We must be very quiet.'

Fear was written all over Father Jacob's face. His hands were shaking, and he jumped in fright at every small noise. Together, they walked through the gates and into the heart of the city. The sleeping buildings cast long moon shadows across the streets. They kept off the main roads, instead, sticking to the dark walkways and alleys. As they headed towards the cathedral, Claude could see the spire in the night sky. The dark clouds above appeared to rotate around it.

They inched their way to the city square and saw the front door was closed, but not chained anymore.

'We have to find a way in, without causing alarm.'

'Around the back, there should be a rectory, a place for the priest to prepare and change.'

Father Jacob bent forward and ran through the dark night until he reached the side of the cathedral. This close, it was extremely grandiose and breathtaking. The ancient stones felt cold as Claude pushed his back against it. Father Jacob waited a moment and held his breath. Then he slid along the side until he reached the far end. Claude followed. A small lowset commode branched off from the cathedral. Claude felt along the old wood panels until he found a door. He tugged on it, but it was locked. Father Jacob pushed it once, twice, then stood back a few steps and ran forward, bursting through it and sending the door showering to the floor in pieces. He stepped inside gingerly and let out a gasp. Several large shelves were covered in dusty, moth-eaten sheets. In the dark they looked like haunting giants. Claude followed Father Jacob through the crowded room until they reached another door. This one wasn't locked, but Claude thought Father Jacob was about to bash it down to tinder also, instead he turned the handle and peered in.

There was a small room that led straight out to the ambulatory area. The soft chatter of talking and humming came through the entrance hall. Father Jacob kept low and hid behind the lower stage, trying to hear what they were saying. Claude crept to the side of the stage and peered around the choir stands. In the middle of the transept floor, the pews had been pushed to the side and there stood Ives Aries, leaning over a large concrete tomb. On the floor behind him, was Abraham. He was tied with filthy rope. His nose was bleeding, and he wasn't moving. Ives was holding an ancient book. The leather-bound tome was draped in cobwebs and covered in dust. He used his finger to trace the words, reading loudly and humming, while tapping a wand on crudely drawn diagrams.

'He's performing the ritual,' Father Jacob said, listening with great intent.

'What do we do?' Claude whispered, turning his head towards him.

Ives sung a verse from the book and the crypt before him started to shake and glow with an eerie yellow light. The crypt moaned like a ship's foghorn on a cloudless night. He slammed the book shut and looked pleased with himself. He walked down from the sepulchre, tucking the wand into his gown and picked up a bag that was laying on the floor. He encircled the unconscious Abraham and poured what appeared to be salt around him in a perfect circle. When he was done, he tossed the salt bag to the side and looked towards the west door entrance. From the dark came several figures. They were dragging two more people behind them. They were slumped by the piled-up pews without care. Claude almost let out a gasp of horror; it was Mabel and Avery Featherstone.

CHAPTER SIXTEEN
DUST AND WORMS

From the depths of the now silent cathedral, came Brother Bishop brandishing a blade. An array of colours splashed across his face as the moon shone through the stained-glass windows of the cathedral. It lit the ground in blues and reds, casting long hues of light along the side isles and nave. Claude recognised the blade instantly as the one Avery had shown him in the storeroom earlier.

'The sacrifices have arrived, Arch Mage Julius Oghast!' Ives screamed as he raised his hands into the air. 'You may rise!'

The top of the catacomb was dead still. Beams of canary yellow light shone out through the ancient cracks. Then, it started to vibrate. The lid of the crypt suddenly started to move on its own. It slid off onto the ground with an ear-deafening thud. Brother Bishop marched forward, his eyes icy white, and handed the long knife to Ives. Claude turned to Father Jacob.

'They are going to sacrifice Mabel and Avery, we have to do something,' he held fear in his voice.

'You free them, I'll get the knife away from Ives. It's the key to putting life back into Julius Oghast.'

One of Ives's masked minions started to light the stakes situated around the cathedral. The dim, dark, church suddenly became an array of dancing lights. Ives walked around the circle waving the blade from side to side, watching as something began to move from deep inside the concrete coffin. A hand suddenly latched onto the side. Its flesh was soft and corroded from age and insects. Its fingernails were yellowed and split.

Claude couldn't wait any longer. He crawled through the choir bleaches on his belly, moving slowly and steadily towards the side isles. There were two small chambers on each side of the transept known as the transept chapels. In order to get to it, Claude would have to traverse through the main rectangular room that cuts across the axis of the cathedral, from there he could reach the Featherstones. Father Jacob went through the other side of the choir arena, moving haphazardly and kneeling beside the crypt.

'Rise, Mage Oghast!' Ives chanted, kneeling down on one knee. He pulled the black wand from his cloak and tapped it inside the circle three times. The wand started to crack down the spine. Ives stared at it as chips fell from it onto the ground before him. It hissed and spat blue embers. He gripped it tightly with both hands and tapped the wand again. It pulled from his hands and spun around the salt circle on its own, before stopping at the foot of the crypt, cracked into three pieces and emitting thick plumes of smoke.

'No!' Ives screamed.

A rotten, ragged figure started to rise up from the centuries old tomb. Its head appeared first, shrouded in a headpiece made of gold and silver. Although it was covered in dust and worms, the gold kept its unique colouring. Where the eyes should have been, were empty hollow sockets. In their place was a void of dark swirling vortexes. Several heavy chains were looped around its neck, pulling at the brittle bones.

'I am weak,' Oghast stated. Its voice as heavy and crackling as distant thunder.

'Yes, Mage Oghast... we have brought you two sacrifices.' The wand should have given Oghast enough life to lift his body from the crypt, however, something had gone wrong and Ives cursed himself for Abraham's sly sabotage.

Claude slipped through the dark and into the transept chapels. In the small square room off the main hall, it was completely void of light. He moved with the shadows until he was close enough to Avery. She had a cloth wrapped around her mouth and her hands and feet were tied. Her hair was dishevelled, and she looked very mad.

'Avery,' Claude said, as softly as he could. She turned to him and mumbled her stifled surprise. 'Shhh,' he said, quietening her. 'I'll untie you and you get yourself and your mother out of here.' She nodded her agreement.

'First,' Ives stated, picking up the knife. 'I must spill the blood of the wandmaker with the blade of Holy Decree. His very essence will feed you power and you shall be whole again, then, you shall feast.'

Oghast faulted as he tried to stand, his body too

frail. Ives held the knife high into the air and chanted in Latin. Suddenly, the blade began to glow bright blue. Shards of magical energy coursed from it like thick, sludgy sparks. Father Jacob ran from beside the coffin, grabbing Ives around the waist and wrestling him to the ground. Ives's masked men stayed where they were, as if possessed to only obey instructions. Father Jacob clutched at the blade but was knocked onto his back. The air was sent from his lungs and he gasped. Ives leapt on top of him. His gnarled face a grimace of hate and destruction.

Claude undid the ropes around Avery's hands and legs. She turned to her mother and started untying hers, just as one of the masked men glanced down. Claude jumped on him before he had a chance to act, knocking him backwards into the huddled pews. Avery leapt to her feet, untying her mother's wrists and joining Claude in the fray. They pinned the man down as best they could, but he was too strong and pushed them off.

Father Jacob grabbed Ives around the neck and held onto him so he couldn't stand. They fell in a heap and rolled around on the ground. Ives freed himself and struck Father Jacob across the face. His eyes rolled into the back of his head and he slumped backward against the wall. Ives turned to the circle of salt. In their tandem melee, one of them had crossed the salt line, destroying it. Standing in the middle, was Abraham. He was battered and bruised and holding his ribs, which felt broken.

'Ives Aries,' he said through gritted teeth.

'Abraham Crenshaw, the lonely wandmaker. It is too late; the great Mage has risen!'

From behind them, Julius Oghast was gaining his footing. Once colourful tunics swathed over his shoulders, now faded and eaten by worms, hung from his skeletal corpse.

'Kill him,' Oghast ordered. 'Drain his blood.'

Ives picked up the blade by his feet and it started to pulsate with cobalt blue light once more. Abraham was weak, but lunged forward, snatching at the knife, but Ives was too strong and knocked him to the ground. He leant over Abraham's crumpled body.

'It has come to an end, old friend,' he said as he raised the blade high above his head.

Claude snatched a flaming torch resting in its handle by the pews and bolted towards Ives as he swung the blade down towards Abraham. The blue glowing blade was struck by the fiery stake as Claude swung at it, hitting it with all his might. He landed, still holding the flaming torch. Embers filled the air as the blade rattled across the ancient wood floor, knocked from Ives's grip. Claude ran to it and snubbed the flame into the blade, just as Avery had shown him with the lantern. The glowing blue energy was extinguished.

Ives screamed and turned towards Julius Oghast. The arch mage opened his rotten mouth and silently roared into the open cathedral. The windows all smashed inwards, showering the floor in an array of stained shards of glass. The mage slumped back into its crypt, lifeless and dead once more.

'No!' Ives screamed standing up on wobbly legs. He spun around to see Abraham standing, with the help of Father Jacob. Both their eyes flashed yellow. 'I'll be back, I promise you that,' he snarled, his body began jerking and shaking wildly as his skin started to grow fur. His ears elongated and he dove to the ground on all fours as long nails protruded from his fingers. His nose turned into a snout and his clothes tore from his body revealing himself as a bear. He stepped forward, roared and leapt towards the window, knocking out the remaining glass and running into the night.

Claude rushed to Abraham and embraced him.

'I'm okay, lad.' His shirt was soaked in blood.

'I'll get the Doctor,' Claude insisted.

'No, lad. Get me home.'

Mabel and Avery had made their way outside and were sitting on the steps of the cathedral, they were both shaken from the event. Brother Bishop was with them.

'I don't remember what happened,' Brother Bishop stated. 'The last thing I remember is that man with the knife coming into my rectory.'

'Take Mabel and Avery home, Brother Bishop. The hour is late, and it has been an eventful night.'

Father Jacob looked back at the damage in the cathedral. 'This will raise questions, Abraham Crenshaw.'

'Yes' he replied. 'We will tell them the truth about Ives Aries and his plans.'

Together they rode in the wagon as the sun was peeking over the distant mountains.

CHAPTER SEVENTEEN
TODAY IS THE DAY

Claude had held the wand up to the light coming through the rear window. He took it back to the work bench and used sandpaper to remove a blemish in the wood. He looked at it again, marvelling at the perfectly shaped wand. He dipped it in the treatment oil and hung it up with the others. Six in total, all hung from hooks along the wall. Abraham came down the stairs, counting coins in his hands.

'Today is the day, lad.'

Claude turned to him. His woodwork apron was too big for his small body. His stitches had been removed from his chest and had started to heal. Abraham's facial injuries and stomach wound were healing also. Claude had nearly forgotten that today was the day he was going to go home. He took his apron off and hung it on the hook. Abraham handed him his payment.

'I will see you in a few days, we have much work to do.'

Claude nodded and felt tears well up in his eyes. 'I'll be back as soon as possible.'

'No, lad. I know your father is ill. It's important to be with your folks.'

'Before you go, I have something for you,' Abraham said, searching in his office. He returned with a box and handed it to Claude.

Claude opened it and inside were a brand-new pair of boots, much like Abrahams. Claude beamed with excitement and tried them on. They fit perfectly. Abraham held his hand out and Claude took it, they shook and looked at each other, smiling.

Claude gathered a small sack of belongings and began his journey. On the path, he had time to process what had happened, and what he had seen. There were things he had learnt that were beyond the understanding of most people. In time he would understand more, but for now, he wanted to see his mother and father.

As he approached the outskirts of Yorktown, he began to run.

THE END

BOOK II
THE WANDMAKER'S LEGACY

*What secret does Abraham hold? Is he able to be trusted?
Abraham and Claude travel to a seaside town to
investigate a series of Dark Magic users. Are they walking
into a trap?
Join Abraham and Claude as the story deepens in the
Wandmaker's Legacy.*

ACKNOWLEDGEMENTS

Thank you to all the authors that have inspired me to keep writing, to show that it is possible. Sabrina and Ouroborus for keeping the dream alive. All the people that edit my books, sorry for the endless work. My family, who are my number one supporters.

For more information on Mitchell visit
www.ouroborusbooks.com

www.ingramcontent.com/pod-product-compliance
Lightning Source LLC
Chambersburg PA
CBHW020231120726
47903CB00008B/2629